I0609621

George Sand

Handsome Lawrence

A sequel to a rolling stone

George Sand

Handsome Lawrence
A sequel to a rolling stone

ISBN/EAN: 9783337385873

Printed in Europe, USA, Canada, Australia, Japan

Cover: Foto ©Andreas Hilbeck / pixelio.de

More available books at **www.hansebooks.com**

NDSOME LAWREN

A

SEQUEL TO "A ROLLING STONE."

BY

GEORGE SAND.

TRANSLATED FROM THE FRENCH

BY

CARROLL OWEN.

BOSTON:
JAMES R. OSGOOD AND COMPANY,
LATE TICKNOR & FIELDS, AND FIELDS, OSGOOD, & CO.
1871.

Entered according to Act of Congress, in the year 1871,

BY JAMES R. OSGOOD & CO.,

In the Office of the Librarian of Congress, at Washington.

UNIVERSITY PRESS: WELCH, BIGELOW, & CO.,
CAMBRIDGE.

HANDSOME LAWRENCE.

I.

LAWRENCE had been speaking for two hours, and the sympathy with which he inspired me made me take a lively interest in his adventures; however, I bethought myself that he must be weary, and I carried him off to dine at my inn, where, having recruited his strength, he likewise resumed his story.

We left off (said he) at my departure for Italy, with Bellamare's company.

Before quitting Toulon I assisted at a closing entertainment, which seemed very strange to me. When the public were pleased with a troupe that had remained some time, they showed their gratitude, and bade them adieu, by throwing presents upon the stage. There was everything, from bouquets to tobacco. Each trade furnished a sample of its industry, — cloths, stockings, cotton caps, household utensils, provisions, shoes, hats, fruit, cutlery, I know not what more. The stage was covered with them, and some were caught in the air, by the musicians, who did not return them. I need not tell you that this patriarchal custom is almost obsolete at the present day.

All went well at the beginning of our journey.

Bellamare, sacrificing his impatience to proceed, consented to travel through Italy, where we made, this time, several short stays tolerably profitable. We played there *L'Aventurière, Il ne faut jurer de rien, Les Folies Amoureuses, Le Verre d'Eau, La Vie de Bohème, Adrienne Lecouvreur, Un Duel sous Richelieu, La Corde Sensible, Jobin et Nanette;* I forget what others. At this period M. Scribe, who was going out of fashion in France, was all the vogue abroad, and, in some small places, we put at the head of the poster the names of Scribe and Melesville to pass off the works of Molière or Beaumarchais. Also, to create a relish for the burlesque songs which Marco sang between the acts, we were forced to compromise the names of Béranger and Désaugiers.

At Florence an adventure happened to me whose memory produced no more impression on me than the passing of a dream. This surprises you; but when you know the events which occurred in rapid succession, on the day after this experience, you will understand why it was not deeply stamped upon my mind.

At the moment of our leaving that city I received the following note:—

I have applauded you both; be happy with HER.

THE UNKNOWN.

I begged Bellamare to tell me if, during our sojourn at Florence, he had seen the Countess. He assured me that he had not, and, as he never gave his word falsely, that was certain. Florence was not then a town so thickly settled that there would be no chance of success in making inquiries.

"Will you stay?" said Bellamare.

I had already, as they say, my foot in the stirrup, and, although I felt greatly excited, I did not wish to try the adventure.

"You see plainly," replied I, that *she* is still persuaded that I intended to deceive her. I cannot accept this position. I will not accept it."

And I passed it by, not without an effort, I confess, but fancying that I honored myself by my pride.

It had been debated whether we should go to Venice and to Trieste, as in the preceding year; but Fate bends us to her will. A letter from M. Zamorini placed at our disposal a great unsightly boat, dignified by the name of tartan, which would transport us at half price from Ancona to Corfu. There we could give some performances which, on the same condition of a division of proceeds between the contractor and ourselves, would enable us to reach Constantinople.

This craft had a very battered look, and the captain, a sort of Jew, who called himself a Greek, appeared to us more garrulous and obsequious than honest and intelligent; but we had no choice; he had made the bargain with Zamorini, through the medium of another captain at Corfu, who would convey us farther.

We performed at Ancona; and as we were leaving the theatre the master of the *Alcyon* — that was the poetical name of our hideous boat — came to tell us that we must set sail at daybreak. We had reckoned on not starting until the day after; nothing was ready; but he objected that the season was capricious, that we must profit by the favorable wind which was blowing, and not wait for contrary winds, which might delay our departure indefinitely. It was then the last of February.

We warned the women to lock their trunks and to snatch a few hours' sleep. The men of the company busied themselves with transporting all the luggage on board the *Alcyon*. We passed the night so, for this luggage was considerable enough. Besides our costumes and personal effects, we had several pieces of scenery indispensable in those localities where the theatre consists only of its four walls, a certain quantity of tolerably voluminous properties, musical instruments, and a supply of provisions; for we might remain some days at sea, and we had been informed that we should find nothing in certain ports where we should touch, upon the coasts of Dalmatia and Albania.

The captain of the *Alcyon* had a cargo of merchandise that filled all the hold, which forced us to heap up ours upon the deck, — a vexatious circumstance, but fortunate, as the sequel will prove.

At daybreak, worn out with fatigue, we weighed anchor, and, pushed off by a strong north wind, we sailed very rapidly toward Brindisi. Leaving Ancona Thursday, we could hope to be at Corfu the Monday or the Tuesday following.

But the wind changed, toward the evening of our departure, and bore us to the offing with a fearful rapidity. We testified some uneasiness to the captain. His boat did not appear capable of supporting so heavy a sea, and thus crossing the Adriatic at its greatest breadth. He replied that the *Alcyon* was capable of making a voyage round the world, and that, if we did not put into Brindisi, we should touch at the opposite coast, either Ragusa or Antivari. He affirmed that the wind was a little northwest, and tended to increase in that direction. He was mistaken, or he lied. The wind carried us toward the east for nearly forty hours, and, as in spite of a very tiresome pitching, we went with great swiftness, we gained confidence, and instead of resting, we did nothing but laugh and sing, until the following night. Then the wind became contrary, and our pilot assured us that it was a good sign, because, upon the coasts of Dalmatia, almost every night the land wind blew over the sea. We were approaching the shore then, but what shore? We were ignorant, and the crew knew no better than ourselves.

During the evening we only skirted a considerable distance along the coasts, broken into a multitude of little islands, whose sombre apparitions were outlined afar off upon a pallid heaven. The moon set early, and the captain, who had pretended to look out for certain lighthouses, reconnoitred nothing further. The sky grew cloudy, a rolling replaced the pitching, and it seemed to us that our sailors sought to regain the open sea. We lost all patience with them ; we wished to land, no matter where. We had had enough of the sea and of our close vessel. Léon soothed us by telling us that it was better to tack about all night, than to approach the thousand rocks scattered along the Adriatic. We grew resigned. I seated myself by Léon on the bales, and we talked about the necessity of arranging a number of plays for our ensuing campaign. There was less chance than in Italy that we should meet with actors who could reinforce us, and our company seemed to me very limited for the schemes of Bellamare.

"Bellamare counted on me," replied Léon, "for a work of mutilation and perpetual retouching, and I have accepted this horrible task. It is not difficult. Nothing is easier than to spoil a play ; but it is heart-rending, and I feel so gloomy that I would not give a fig for the rest of my life."

I endeavored to console him ; but our conversation was every moment interrupted. The sea became detestable, and the movements of our sailors continually disturbed us. Towards midnight the wind shifted, and they confessed to us that it was impossible to steer with certainty.

The captain began to lose his head ; he lost it completely when a shock, light at first, followed by a second shock more violent, warned us that we struck the reefs. I cannot say if it would have been possible to cast anchor or to try any other manœuvre to save ourselves; however that may be, the crew allowed the *Alcyon* to founder on the rocks. The poor skiff did not frolic there long; a violent collision, succeeded by an ominous creaking, made us swiftly realize that we were lost. The hold began to fill, the prow was broken. We made some fathoms still, and found ourselves at a sudden stand-still, caught between two rocks, on one of which I sprang, bearing Impéria in my arms. My comrades followed my example, and rescued the other women. Well for us that we took thought for them and for ourselves, for the captain and his crew cared only for their cargo, and strove in vain to secure its safety, without concerning themselves with us. The tartan, arrested by the rocks, bounded like a mad animal; its sides resisted still; we had time to save everything on the deck, and after a half-hour devoted to this feverish work, happily crowned with success, the *Alcyon*, lifted up by heavier and heavier surges, freed herself from the narrow passage by a backward bound, as if she wished to make a spring to clear it; then, dashed on anew, she struck it a second time, but half filled with water, the keel crushed, the masts broken. A formidable wave raised up what remained of this miserable structure, and cast upon the rock where we had found a refuge a portion of the flooring and some fragments of the hull; the rest was swallowed up. They could rescue nothing from the contents of the hold.

The island where we found ourselves, and whose name I never knew —perhaps it had none—might measure five hundred yards in length by one hundred in breadth. It was a calcareous rock, white as marble and perpendicular on all sides, save for a cleft where the sea entered and formed a tiny road, strewn with detached blocks, presenting in miniature the appearance of the archipelago of which our rock formed part.

It was thanks to this little opening, where the caprice of the waves had thrown us, that we were able to obtain a footing; but we had at first no leisure to examine narrowly either the inside or the outside of our refuge. At the first moment we thought ourselves on land, and it was with astonishment that we beheld ourselves prisoners upon this isolated rock. As for me, I did not understand at all the danger of our situation; I doubted not for an instant that we could leave it with facility; and while Bellamare made a circuit of it for the purpose of investigation, I sought and found a refuge for the women, a sort of great basin naturally scooped out in the rock, where they could be sheltered from the wind. You may well believe that they were filled with terror and consternation. Impéria, alone, preserved her presence of mind, and endeavored to revive their courage. Régine became devout and said her prayers. Anna had hysterics, and rendered our condition still more lugubrious by piercing cries. It was in vain that Bellamare, intrepid and calm, told her that we were saved. She heard nothing, and only grew quiet before the threats of Moranbois, who spoke of throwing her into the sea. Fear acted on her as on children: she begged pardon, wept, and grew tranquil.

When we were sure that none of us were injured, or failed to answer to their names, for darkness still enveloped us, we wished to consult with the captain upon the means of leaving this unpleasant shelter. "The means?" said he in a despondent tone. "There are none! This is the cruel *bora*, the most pernicious of winds, which is blowing at present, God knows how many days, between the land and us. And then, my dear lords, there is still another thing! The *vila* has enchained us, and whatever we might attempt would turn against us." "The *vila*?" said Bellamare. "Is it another contrary wind? One was surely enough, it seems to me!" "No, no, *signor mio*, it is not a wind; it is even worse; it is the wicked fairy who lures ships upon the breakers, and who laughs to see them broken. Do you hear her? I hear her! It is not the pebbles washed up by the sea. There are no pebbles on these steep coasts. It is the laughter of the infamous *Vila*, her death-boding laugh, her wicked laugh!" "Where are we, say, idiot?" asked Bellamare, shaking the superstitious captain.

The poor wretch understood nothing, and repeated incessantly, "*Scoglio maledetto! pietra del Diavolo!*" So that we were free to apply either of these despairing epithets, by way of a name, to our rock. That did not benefit us. The chief thing was to recognize the shore, in sight of which we found ourselves, and which no lighthouse signalized. The captain asked his men. One answered Zara, the other Spalatro. The captain shrugged his shoulders, declaring it Ragusa.

"Ah well, we are at a stand-still," said Bellamare, laughing ruefully.

"Not quite that," said Moranbois, in his turn. "When we reach the coast, we shall see for a certainty. Why the deuse not make a raft with the fragments of the tartan!"

The captain shook his head; his two men did likewise, seated themselves upon the *débris*, and remained motionless.

"Rouse them, beat them," said Moranbois, swearing. "They shall either speak or obey."

They replied to our threats at last, that we must neither stir, nor show ourselves, nor make any noise, because the wind was going down, and, if we were on the coast of Almissa, whose archipelago was infested with pirates, we should inevitably be robbed and murdered. We must await the daylight; these brigands were bold only at night.

"What!" cried Léon, indignant; "there are ten men of us here, more or less armed, and you fancy that we fear these sea-robbers? Come, then! find your tools speedily, and set about the work. If you refuse to aid us, there is one of our own number who will direct us, and we can do without you."

He pointed to Moranbois, who had lived long enough upon the port of

Toulon to have sufficient knowledge, and who began his work without waiting for the consent of the captain. Léon, Lambesq, Marco, and I received his orders, and worked with energy, while Bellamare occupied himself with collecting and loading the guns. He thought that the fears of the captain were not entirely without foundation, and that our shipwreck might really attract robbers from the shore, if we were far from port.

The captain watched our labors. The loss of his merchandise had completely demoralized him. Fearing the sea less than men, he bewailed himself on seeing us light a torch and hammer loudly on the ruins of the *Alcyon.*

"We must not blind our eyes to it; with this wretched bit of flooring, and these detestable waifs, we cannot make a raft for fifteen persons; if we can accommodate four on it, the sky will fall. However, if the raft will hold only me, I pledge you my word that I will use it to seek assistance."

During a moment of rest, I ran to see what had become of the women. Crowded together like birds in the snow, they shivered with cold, while we were in a perspiration. I urged them to walk about. None of them felt the courage for it, and, for the first time, I saw Impéria dejected.

"Is it possible, you?" I said.

"I think of my father," she replied; "if we should not succeed in leaving here, who will maintain him?"

"I," rejoined I, declaiming a reply taken from a modern drama; "'he shall have the friendship of Beppo, if he escapes!'"

I was gay as a lark; but the remainder of the night must have appeared mortally long to these poor shipwrecked creatures. To us it passed like an instant, and the sun surprised us, working for four hours, without suspecting how the time slipped by. No pirate showed himself; the raft was launched; Moranbois took the command, and installed himself upon it, with the captain and one of the sailors. There was only room for three, and Moranbois would trust to no one but himself to bring us prompt assistance. With emotion we beheld him leap upon this miserable craft, without bidding farewell to any one, or displaying the least anxiety. The sea was furious around the rock; but we perceived, at a considerable distance, a long extent of cliffs, which seemed to us to be the coast of Dalmatia, and we hoped that the passage of our friend would be rapid. We were then surprised to see that the raft, instead of proceeding in that direction, reached the open sea, and soon it disappeared behind the mountainous surges that cut off our horizon. It was because the apparent shore was only a series of rocks, worse than that on which we were stranded. We could convince ourselves of that, when the morning fog had cleared away. We were in a literal alley, surrounded by islands higher than our own, and which entirely screened from us the horizon on the landward side, excepting some peaks of a rosy white which appeared to us from afar off. They were the summits of the Dalmatian Alps, which we had already seen from the coast of Italy, and to which it seemed that crossing of the Adriatic had hardly brought us nearer. The sailor whom they had left with us gave us no information; he spoke only an unintelligible Sclavonic dialect; and as Marco, while at sea, had jeered him somewhat, he would not answer our questions.

On the side toward the open sea we had only narrow vistas, the *Alcyon* being determined to conceal its disaster at all points of the horizon. The splendid chain of submerged mountains which surrounded us presented a spectacle magnificent in horror and heart-sickening in nakedness; not a blade of grass upon the rock, not a sea-weed clinging to its sides; no hope of catching any fish in those clear and deep waters, no chance of passing over the ever-turbulent waves, without assistance from abroad. Ten times we made in vain the tour of our prison, and in vain we consulted our guide-books and our charts. In vain we told ourselves that around the eastern coasts of the Adriatic are scattered habitable islands; there was no trace of life about us.

We were not yet utterly disheartened by this situation. They must sail along all these shores, and it would not be long before small vessels would appear around us; at all events, the raft would soon accost one, and give a signal of our distress.

With the return of the sun the wind had completely changed. It blew from the west with violence,— a disquieting circumstance, all things considered. No fishing-smack would put out to sea, and no sailing vessel would venture within the neighbor-hood of the breakers. Could Moranbois land anywhere without being dashed to pieces? He had stocked his raft with as many provisions as it would contain. What remained to us was not reassuring, and we judged it prudent to delay as long as possible before having recourse to it. The slight tide perceptible in the Adriatic gained the entrance of the basin, and we hoped, Marco and I, that it would bring us shell-fish, with which we resolved to content ourselves, not to break in upon the supply of food.

We watched for the tide to prevent it from carrying back the riches which it might deliver us. It brought us only empty shells. Impéria, who had regained her composure, begged me to collect the prettiest for her. She took them, sorted them, and, seated on an extremity of the rock, she drew from her pocket the little roll of needlework which never left her, and began to string these sorry jewels in a necklace, as if she were preparing to attend a ball that evening. Pale and already wasted from a night of suffering and mortal anguish, dishevelled by the wind, which did not *play* with her locks, but seemed to wish to tear them from her, she was serious and as sweet as I had seen her in the greenroom of the Odéon, recovering from her illness, and already working at her lace, until she should be summoned to perform her part.

"You observe her," said Bellamare, who also contemplated her: "that girl is certainly a round above humanity; she is there like an angel among the damned."

"Are you ill?" I said, regarding him with surprise.

He appeared so changed that I was frightened. He understood, and said with a smile: "You are no less alarming than I; we are all alarming! We are jaded with fatigue. We must eat; otherwise we shall all be mad in ten minutes."

He was right. Lambesq began to pick a quarrel with Marco; and Purpurin, half reclining in the water, recited, with a stupid air, verses which had no meaning.

We hastened to the provisions; they were not damaged, but, furnished by the master of the *Alcyon*, who speculated in everything, they were of very bad quality, except the wine, which was good, and of sufficient quantity for several days. The women were served first. Only one ate with good appetite; this was Régine, who drank proportionately, and, as we had no fresh water, she was soon completely intoxicated, and went to sleep in the corner, where the tide would have swept her away, if we had not led her up a little higher on the cliff.

Lambesq, already overexcited, grew tipsy also, and little Marco, who was still sober, was soon seized with a feverish gayety. The others were more circumspect, and I laid aside a portion of my rations, without any one's perceiving it. I began to think that Moranbois, if he were not swallowed up by the sea or dashed upon the shore, might be long in returning, and I wished to sustain the strength of Impéria, at the expense of my own, until the last hour.

No sail appeared to us during that day, which grew foggy toward noon. The wind sank, and the cold decreased. We busied ourselves with constructing a shelter for the women, breaking up the rock, which was half-way between white marble and chalk, and offered us slight resistance. We hollowed out a sort of grotto, whose size we increased with a little wall of dry stones. We made them a common bed of casks and bales, and covered it with a stage-curtain, which, strange mockery of fate! represented the sea seen through cliffs. Another curtain, fastened to the walls of genuine rock by cords, formed the wardrobe and dressing-room of these ladies.

We occupied ourselves next with establishing a lookout which might rise above the rocks on the side toward the sea. We watched in vain the waves that lashed our prison; they did not bring the slightest fragment of the masts of the *Alcyon*. The frail rollers of our curtains could not resist the feeblest sea-breeze; despite the skill and care which we exerted in securing them, they were blown away after a few moments, and we had to give up planting the signal of distress.

Night overtook us before we could think of constructing any shelter whatever for ourselves. The east wind revived, and blew again very cold and very rough. Three or four times we were forced to replace and secure the tent of the women, who slumbered all the same, except Anna, who awoke, and uttered from time to time a piercing shriek; but the others were too much overpowered to notice it.

We had still some miserable chips left to kindle a fire. Bellamare urged us to husband this resource until the last moment, or in case one of us should become seriously ill. We might be rescued at any moment by the approach of a vessel ; but it was also evident that we might be prisoners as long as the wind forced the ships to keep to the open sea, or while the fog prevented us from being signalled.

The cold became so sharp towards morning, that we all perceived how the fever was gaining on us. We still had some provisions, but no one was hungry, and we tried to warm ourselves with the contents of a cask of Cyprus wine, which assuaged for a space, but soon increased the irritation.

This was, however, only the beginning of our sufferings. The following day brought torrents of rain, at which we rejoiced at first. We could quench our thirst, and put by a little supply of fresh water, in the few vessels which we possessed ; but we were chilled, and, our thirst satisfied, hunger returned with new intensity. Bellamare, seconded by the agreement of Léon, Marco, and myself, decreed that we should resist as long as possible before attacking our last resource.

This second day of fruitless waiting brought to all of us the first idea of a possible abandonment upon this barren rock. The sensation of mental suffering increased our physical evils. We were more dismayed than we had been at the moment of shipwreck. Lambesq grew insupportable from useless complaints and vain recriminations. The sailor who had remained with us, and who was a veritable brute, spoke already, in pantomime, of drawing lots which of us should be eaten.

In the evening, the rain having ceased, we burned, to restore Anna, who fainted continually, what little wood we had. Impéria, whom I had forced to accept the food that I reserved, made her eat it. What remained of our stores disappeared during the night, devoured by Lambesq or by the sailor, perhaps by both. All the fresh water, saved with care, went the same way, or leaked out.

This third night there succeeded to the rain which had drenched our clothing a cold so intense that we could not speak, our teeth chattered so. We split open the box of costumes, and drew out at random whatever it contained in the way of doublets, dresses, pelisses, and cloaks. The women were wet also ; the rain had penetrated both the curtain which served them as *velarium*, and the vault of spongy rock which we had hollowed out for them. This accursed rock did not keep the water that we might have saved in the holes, and it did not protect us.

We wished to burn the chest which had held our finery : Bellamare opposed it. It might serve as a shelter to the last survivor.

At length the third day brought back the sun, and, with the end of the fog, the hope of being perceived. We cheered up a little; we cherished illusions ; Anna regained somewhat of her strength ; intoxication still consoled those who would resort to it. I could not prevent little Marco from exceeding the necessary quantity. He detested Lambesq, whose arrogance and selfishness exasperated him. We had much ado to restrain them from fighting in good earnest.

A sudden hope of safety diverted us; we perceived, at last, a sail upon the horizon! We made what signals we could. Alas! it was too far off, and we were too small, too much hidden by the rocks! It passed. A second, a third, then two others, toward evening, threw us, first into a delirious excitement, and then into a hopeless dejection. Anna slept so soundly that it was impossible to awaken her, to induce her to eat some shell-fish which we had succeeded in catching. Lucinde put her head in her shawl, and remained as if petrified. Régine began her devotions again; a livid pallor had replaced the purplish red of intoxication on her face. We were forced to secure Purpurin, to prevent him from throwing himself into the sea, and to keep the sailor quiet by main force, since he rushed at us to drink our blood.

Thirst began to torture us again; the Cyprus wine only irritated it, and there were moments when, the brute gaining the ascendency, I had to entreat Bellamare and Léon, still masters of themselves, to prevent me from drinking myself to death.

Should we have suffered less without this wine, which set our blood on fire, and devoured our famished vitals? It may be; but it may be, too, that we should have perished from the cold and damp, before receiving assistance.

The hut that we had built protected us but little. The chest for costumes was large enough to contain one person, crouching down. Lambesq took possession of it, and, cowering within this refuge, he showered abuse and threats on any one who approached him, such was his fear of being dispossessed of it. In the endeavor to shut the cover over him, at the risk of suffocating, he broke it and cursed so much the more.

"It serves you right," Bellamare said to him; "selfish people gain nothing. You will do well to survive us, for if it is another who is destined to this sad advantage, he certainly will not compose your funeral eulogy."

To escape Lambesq's sour reply, he withdrew me to a little distance, and said to me: "My dear boy, what we suffer here is nothing, if we can leave this rock. I will not doubt it; but I should speak falsely, if I said that I felt sure of it; and even if the fact were evident, I could not shake off the profound grief which the more than probable death of Moranbois causes me. It is the first time in my life that sadness is stronger than my will. You are young, you have courage and energy. Léon is a silent stoic; Marco is an excellent lad, but too young for such a trial. So it is for you to give me courage, if I lack it. Will you promise me to be the *man* and head of our poor shipwrecked family, if Bellamare is brought low by death or by delirium?"

"You are ingenious," I answered, "in instruction as in everything else. I understand. At the moment when

I was giving way, you find means to restore me, by feigning to give way also. Thanks, my friend, I will strive, even till the last hour, to be worthy of seconding you."

He embraced me, and I perceived tears on the cheeks of this man, whom, hitherto, I had always seen laughing.

"Let me weep like a fool," replied he, with his accustomed smile, now grown heart-rending. "Moranbois will have no other farewell than these tears from a friend, perhaps soon departed likewise. This rude companion of my wandering life was devotion personified. He will have died as he ought to die! Let us try, also, to die worthily, my child, if we must remain upon this rock which prolongs our agony. It would have been easy to perish by sinking with the boat. To succumb to thirst and cold is longer and harder. Let us be men, come! Let us abstain from this wine that exhilarates and weakens us; I am sure of it. I have read accounts of shipwrecks, and the record of those who have committed suicide by starvation. I know that hunger ceases at the end of three or four days; we have reached that limit; in three or four days more thirst also will have disappeared; and those of us who have good constitutions may live still for several days, without madness or suffering. Let us prepare, by hope and patience, to sustain the weaker ones, the women especially. Anna is the most nervous, hence she will .resist the best. It is the most courageous, it is Impéria, who gives me most anxiety, because she forgets herself for the others, and no longer thinks to preserve herself from anything. Know that I have a treasure concealed about me, and that I am reserving it for her, — a box of dates, very small, alas! and a vial of fresh water. We must not wait for her first symptom of weakness; for with those natures which fall only to die, a late assistance is superfluous. Go and bring her for me, and when we have her here we will force her to eat and drink."

I hastened to obey, without telling Impéria what was the matter. We led her to the extremity of the island, and there Bellamare said to her: "My child, you will obey, or I give you my word of honor that I will throw myself into the sea. I will not see you starve."

"I am not hungry," she answered. "I suffer from nothing; it is I who will throw myself into the sea, if you do not both eat what remains."

She refused, obstinately, affirming that she was strong, and could still wait a long time. While speaking thus, with animation, she suddenly fainted. Some drops of water revived her, and when she was better, we obliged her, with an almost brutal authority, to eat some dates.

"Will you not eat some too?" she asked us in a tone of entreaty.

"Remember your father," I said to her; "it is not permitted you to renounce your life."

The next day, which was the fourth, it was magnificent weather again, and we warmed ourselves in the sun. Weakness began to overpower us all; we were quiet, we had no more wine. Lambesq and the sailor slept, at last, profoundly. Purpurin had lost his memory, and no longer recited verses. Bellamare, Léon, Marco, and I entered the little enclosure reserved for the women. Impéria had succeeded in reanimating them by her unalterable patience. She sustained her companions as Bellamare did his.

"Stay with us," she said to us, "we are no longer either sick or gloomy, see! We have dressed ourselves, and arranged our hair; we have put our drawing-room in order, and receive our friends. At present, it seems impossible to us that assistance should not arrive to-day, the weather is so fine! Régine, who became a saint, through fear of dying, persuades herself that she is fasting voluntarily, to atone for her former sins. Lucinde has found her mirror again, mislaid in moving, and is convinced that pallor is very becoming to her. She has even decided to whiten her paint, when she ascends the stage again. Our little Anna is recovered, and we have concluded to talk, as if between the acts, without remembering that we are not here for our pleasure."

"Ladies," replied Bellamare, very gravely, "we accept your gracious invitation, but on condition that your programme shall be serious. I propose that we demand a forfeit from the one who shall speak of the sea, or the wind, or the rock, or hunger and thirst, in short, of anything that may recall the disagreeable accident that detains us here."

"Agreed!" cried everybody.

And we begged Léon to recite some verses of his own composition.

"No," replied he, "my verses are always sad. I have always regarded my life as a shipwreck, and we must not speak of it here. It would be in the worst taste; the thing is decided."

"Ah well," responded Bellamare, "we will have a little music. The box of instruments is with you, ladies; it serves you as a bed, if I mistake not: open it, and let each do what he can."

He gave me the violin, and took the bass-viol; Marco seized upon the cymbals, and Léon the flute; we were all something of musicians, for, in the localities where they did not understand French, we sang the comic opera very passably; and when musicians were lacking for the orchestra, one of us directed the amateurs, and performed his part.

The effect of our concert was to plunge us all in tears. It was like a general signal. Purpurin, attracted by the music, came to embrace his master's knees, telling him that he would go with him to the end of the world.

"To the end of the world!" replied Bellamare, in a melancholy tone; "it seems to me that is exactly where we are!"

"A forfeit!" cried Impéria; "we are to make no allusions here. Purpurin has spoken well: we will all go to the end of the world, and we will return from it."

Then she began to sing and dance, taking us by the hand, and we followed her example, without remembering anything, and without perceiving the weakness of our legs; but, a few moments after, we were all lying asleep upon the rock.

I awoke first. Impéria was near

me. I seized her in my arms, and embraced her passionately, without knowing what I did.

"What is it, then?" she asked me, in alarm; "what is happening to us now?"

"Nothing," I answered, "except that I feel I am dying, and that I will not die, without having told the truth. I adore you; it was for you that I became an actor. You are all the world to me, and I shall love but you throughout eternity."

I know not what I said to her beside; I was delirious. It seemed to me as if I had talked to her a long time, and with a loud voice, which awoke no one. Bellamare, attired as Crispin, lay inert and motionless beside us; Léon, in Russian costume, had his head upon the knees of Marco, enveloped in a Roman toga. I regarded them with stupefaction.

"See," said I to Impéria, "the play is finished! all the characters are dead: it is a burlesque drama; we are going to die, also, you and I. That is why I tell you the secret, the great secret of my rôle and of my life. I love you, I love you madly. I love you so that I am dying of it, and I die!"

She made no answer, but began to weep. I became insane.

"It must be finished," I said, laughing.

And I wished to throw her into the sea, but I lost consciousness, and of the two days that followed I have preserved only a vague remembrance. There was no longer either gayety or anger or sadness; we were all dull and indifferent. The sea brought us some waifs, covered with miserable barnacles, which kept us from starving, and which we picked up with a surprising indolence, we were so sure of perishing, notwithstanding. A few drops of rain fell, and hardly assuaged our thirst; some even did not wish to profit by these slight alleviations, which awoke again the slumbering desire for life. I recall my impressions with difficulty, and I remember only certain returns of my fixed idea. Impéria was continually in my dreams, for I was continually asleep; when Bellamare, who still resisted this languor, came to arouse me a little, I could no longer distinguish between fiction and reality, and, thinking that he summoned me for the performance, I asked him my opening cue; or else I fancied that I was with him in the famous blue chamber, and I addressed him in a low voice. I believe that I revealed my love to Impéria again, and that she understood me no longer. She made lace, or thought to make it; for her fingers, rigid and transparent from emaciation, often worked in the empty air. One morning, I know not how long after, I felt that some one, who was very strong, raised me up, and carried me off, like a child. I opened my eyes, and found my face close to a sunburned visage, that I kissed, without knowing why, for I did not recognize it: it belonged to Moranbois.

We had passed seven nights and six days on the rock, between life and death. I cannot tell you what happened to me, from my personal impressions, for I was completely stupid and almost idiotic for a week. The most of my companions suffered the same consequence from our misfortunes; but I will keep you to the regular course of my narration, according to what I learned from Bellamare and Moranbois, as I gradually recovered health and reason.

The last night of our martyrdom on the *accursed rock*, Bellamare had been startled out of his sleep by the sailor, who wished to strangle him, that he might devour him. He defended himself, and the struggle had resulted in his enemy's being plunged into the sea. He had not reappeared, and no one had lamented him: only Lambesq had expressed some regret that, as Bellamare had killed him in a case of lawful self-defence, he should have given up the wretch's remains to the fishes. Lambesq did not recoil in the least from the idea of eating a fellow-creature, little appetizing as he might be, and, had he felt sufficient strength, I know not what attempt he might have made against us.

But it is Moranbois's campaign in which you will be interested. This is what happened to him, from the time of his departure, when he embarked upon the raft.

Scarcely had he left the surges that lashed the rocks so furiously, when he found himself swept out into the open sea, by an extraordinary and wholly inexplicable current. The master of the *Alcyon* could not understand it, and said that within the memory of man such a thing had never been seen upon the Adriatic. On gaining the land, where, after twenty hours of desperate endeavor, he arrived alone, dashed upon the rocks with the fragments of the raft, and the corpses of his two companions, our friend comprehended what had occurred. An earthquake, of which we had been unconscious at the moment of our shipwreck, had filled the coasts of Delmatia with consternation, and, changing perhaps the submarine conformation of the reefs where we were stranded, had produced a sort of tidal wave, which lasted several days.

Moranbois himself had been cast upon a sterile island, inhabited by fishermen belonging to Ragusa. He was half dead when they found him. It was some hours before he could explain himself by signs, for they did not understand a word either of French or Italian. All he could obtain from them was to be conducted to another island, where he experienced the same obstacles in making himself understood, the same difficulty in gaining the mainland. You know that this country was formerly laid waste by furious earthquakes, one of which even destroyed, from top to bottom, the splendid city of Ragusa, the modern Venice as it was then called. Moranbois found the dwellers on the sea-shore much more terrified for themselves than eager to go to the assistance of others. He dragged himself as far as Gravosa, which is the suburb and war-port of Ragusa, and there, overcome by weariness, sorrow, and vexation, he was so ill that they carried him to the hospital, where he expected to die, without being able to save us.

When he could leave his bed, and talk with the local authorities, they took him for a madman, he was so excited by fever and despair. His story appeared improbable, and they spoke of confining him. You may imagine that his language, habitually unconventional, had acquired, under such circumstances, an energy which did not prepossess them in his favor. They suspected him of wishing to carry off a vessel, for a pretended search for shipwrecked people, in order to deliver it into the hands of pirates. There was even a question of imprisoning him, for having assassinated the captain of the *Alcyon*. At last, when he had succeeded in proving his sincerity, and the weather had grown calmer, he managed to secure, at any price, a vessel whose crew jeered at him, and conducted him in the adventure, without haste, and without consenting to approach the rocks, precisely where he wished to land. He tacked about a long time, before recognizing the place where we were, and could only reach it with a life-boat, with which he had provided himself.

All this explains to you why he did not arrive until the moment when we had given up both the hope and the desire to struggle. I must except Bellamare, whose clear recollections proved to us that he had not ceased for an instant to watch over us and notice our condition.

The boat conveyed us to the port of Ragusa, and it was there that, after several days had elapsed, I regained my memory of the past and my consciousness of the present. We had all been very ill, but, with my strong young frame, robust, and consequently exacting much nourishment, I had been more exhausted than the others. Moranbois recov-

ered in two days; Anna was still so weak that she had to be carried; Lambesq was better than any of us, physically, but his mind was much confused, and he continued to believe himself on the rock, and to bewail himself stupidly. Lucinde swore that she would never again leave the rustic stage, and, glued to her mirror, tormented herself about the length of her nose, rendered more apparent by the wasting of her cheeks. Régine, on the contrary, was not sorry to lose flesh, and still found food for her mirth, more particularly for her cynicism; she had made progress in this respect. Léon had preserved his reason, but his liver troubled him, and, without complaining, he appeared more misanthropic than formerly. Marco, on the other hand, was more considerate and affectionate, speaking only of the others, and forgetful of himself. Purpurin had become almost dumb from stupefaction, and Moranbois fervently desired he might remain so.

As for Impéria, who interested me more than all the others, she was mysterious in illness as in all things; she had suffered less, physically, than her companions, owing to the slight sustenance that Bellamare had forced her to accept; but her mind seemed to have undergone a peculiar disturbance. She had been less ill, but she was more affected, and could not bear the least allusion to past sufferings.

"She was sublime to the very last," said Bellamare to me, when I expressed my surprise to him; "she thought only of us, nothing of herself. Now, there is a reaction; she pays for her excessive devotion; she has taken a little distaste to all of us, for having caused her too much fatigue and anxiety. In proportion as I saw her sweet and patient with the sufferers that we were, she now feels exacting and irritable with the convalescents that we are; she is not conscious of it. Let us seem as if we did not perceive it. In a few days the equilibrium will be recovered. Dame Nature is an implacable ruler; devotion overcomes her, but she resumes her rights when this great stimulant no longer needs to act."

Impéria did, indeed, regain her equilibrium in a little while, except with me. She seemed distrustful of me; at times she was even critical and sarcastic. She overcame it, when she saw me surprised and grieved, but the friendship and familiarity of old had ceased. What had passed, then, during my days of delirium? I could recall only what I have told you. It was certainly enough to put her on her guard against me; but had she understood it? could she remember it? might she not attribute my passion to the fever that was then devouring me? I dared not question her for the very fear of reminding her of a fact perhaps forgotten. I, also, assumed the carelessness of former times. I was too weak to feel in love, and I liked to persuade myself that I had never been so. It is certain that we were all singularly wasted and indifferent. When we were all assembled again, for the first time, upon the terrace of a little villa that we had rented on the wooded hill which overlooks the port, it was not the thinness and pallor of their faces that struck me; they were less appalling than they had been on the rock; it was an expression common to all, and which established a sort of family resemblance on the most dissimilar features. Our eyes were large and prominent, as if frightened, and, in piteous contrast, a stupid smile parted our trembling lips. We all had a sort of stammer and more or less deafness. Some of them even felt the effects a long time after.

Bellamare, who had not rested a moment, watching over us all, superintending the prescriptions of the physicians of the country, who did not inspire him with confidence, himself administering to us the medicines of his portable dispensary, began to feel fatigue when ours was disappearing. We had been in this little port for five days, upon a charming coast, in view of fine mountains, of a bluish gray, which bounded it, and none of us was yet in a condition to work or to travel. Since leaving Ancona, that is to say, for nearly a month, we had earned nothing, and had expended a considerable sum. Bellamare, having nothing, wished to economize during our convalescence. The financial situation grew worse every day, and every day, likewise, the brow of Moranbois darkened; but he did not wish to speak of it, fearing that, in organizing performances at Ragusa, Bellamare would devote himself too soon to fresh cares and fatigues. Was there a theatre at Ragusa? We had saved our curtains for the background, and Léon applied himself to the task of repainting them, while Marco and I occupied our leisure in relining them. I troubled myself about nothing. I had still my little fortune of bank-notes in my belt, and I regarded it as equivalent to the safety of the troupe and manager, when their funds should be entirely exhausted. But they were not yet to owe this safety to me. One evening, as we were sipping coffee in the orchard, under the citron-trees, all in blossom, they announced to us the visit of the proprietor of the villa, who was also the owner of the craft that Moranbois had hired to go in search of us. Nothing had as yet been paid.

"Prepare for quarter of an hour of Rabelais," Bellamare said to us, as he looked at Moranbois, who was swearing under his breath.

"Have no uneasiness," said I, "I am still in funds; let us receive the creditor politely."

A tall young man appeared, bound round the waist like a wasp, glittering with purple and gold, beautiful in face as the antique, and full of majestic grace, in his rich military costume.

"Which of you, gentlemen," he said, in good French, and with a courteous bow, "is the manager of the troupe?"

"I am," replied Bellamare, "and I have to thank you for the confidence with which the keeper of this villa authorized me, in your name, to instal myself here with my poor shipwrecked and still invalid company, without requiring any deposit from me; but we are proportionately —"

"That is no matter," responded this brilliant personage; "I do not let this house, I lend it. I do not make shipwrecked people pay for the relief which every man owes his fellow-creature."

"But, monsieur —"

"Say nothing more about it, it would offend me. I am Prince Klémenti, wealthy for my country, — what would be poverty in yours, where they have other needs and other customs and also other expenses. Everything is relative. I was educated in France, at the College Henri IV. So I am a little civilized and a little French; my mother was a Parisian. I love the theatre, of which I have been long deprived, and I consider artists as clever and cultivated people, who are very necessary to our progress. The only object of my visit is to take you away to pass the spring among our mountains, where you will speedily recover, in a healthful climate, amid a spirited people, who will be charmed by your talents, and who, like me, will regard themselves as your debtors, when you have taken up your abode among them."

Bellamare, won by this gracious invitation, consulted us in regard to it, and, seeing himself generally supported, he promised to comply with the prince's request, for some days only, as soon as we were in a condition to act and sing again.

"No, no," replied the handsome Klémenti. "I am not willing to wait. I wish to take you away, give you rest and comfort with me, all the time you require; you shall perform only when you please, and not at all, if you prefer. I still consider you only as shipwrecked persons, in whom I am interested, and whom I wish to make my friends, until they become my artists."

Léon, who was not fond of patrons, brought forward the objection that we were expected at Constantinople, and that we had made engagements.

"With whom?" cried the prince; "with M. Zamorini?"

"Precisely."

"Zamorini is a rascal, who means to make money out of you, and leave you without resources in the streets of Constantinople. Last year, at Bucharest, I met an Italian lady whom he had taken for a *prima donna*, and abandoned in that city, where she was earning her bread as a servant in the inn; had it not been for me, she would be there still. Now, she is singing successfully at Trieste. She was an accomplished person, who has preserved her friendship for me, and whom I have restored to liberty, after asking a few singing-lessons from her. Of you I will ask only to chat with me from time to time, to polish me up, and perfect me in my French, which I am afraid of forgetting. When you are all quite well, you shall resume your flight, if you insist on it, and if you desire to visit our enemies, the Turks, I will facilitate your journey; but I should be greatly surprised if Zamorini has not failed before now. There was a very handsome woman who built up his business, when he went under. She grew tired of being cheated by this wretch, and left him, to try her fortune in Russia, three months ago."

The handsome prince continued to converse, with that readiness of language which is peculiar to the Sclavonic races; for he was not Albanian, as we had been led to believe from the similarity of his dress to that worn by this nation. He called himself Montegrine, but he was properly of Herzegovinian or Bosnian lineage. What was very amusing, these ancestors, whose portraits we saw, erelong, at his residence, had the square and bony features of the Hungarians, and he owed his handsome Greek type to his mother, who, as we knew later, was a milliner from the Rue Vivienne, and no more Greek than you or I. This personage, so unreserved and perfectly amiable on the surface, attracted nearly all of us; and as he assured us that his principality was only a day's journey from Ragusa, we yielded to the desire that he expressed to take us thither the day following.

As the roadstead of Gravosa runs very far into the land, we re-embarked with all our material, in the tartan which had brought us, the prince performing its honors with much graciousness. He did not seem to notice that the interior was not as clean as it might have been,— a circumstance that afforded us some insight into the customs of the country. For the rest, this vessel, which the prince rarely used, and which at other times was engaged, for his benefit, in the coasting-trade, did not lack pretension, when it conveyed His Highness. It was then covered with a party-colored tent, which was furnished with a sort of roof, scalloped and decorated in the style of the fairy-scenes of our Boulevards. It is true that this ornamentation seemed to have passed through the hands of a decorator of Carpentras.

They landed us, so that we could take a carriage to Ragusa, where a plentiful breakfast awaited us, and where we were allowed to visit the palace of the Doges, before re-entering our hired carriages. At last we turned in the direction of the mountains, by a fine shady road which ascended quite gradually, and which, at every winding, showed us a charming country. We had once more grown gay, careless, prepared for anything. Travelling on *terra firma* was our element: all our troubles faded like a dream.

But, at the end of a short passage, farther on, behold a frightful perpendicular pathway! The carriages are paid for and dismissed. The boxes and stage properties are consigned to people who will transport them in their arms in two days. Mules, led by women in picturesque rags, await us on the summit of the mountain, which we must ascend on foot. I did so with pleasure, for my part, feeling that my legs, so far from refusing to serve me, grew stronger at every step; but I dreaded for Bellamare and Impéria the remainder of a journey which did not appear to be strewn with flowers.

It was, in reality, very painful. In the first place, our women were frightened at finding themselves perched upon mules, in dizzy paths, and intrusted to other women, who never ceased to laugh and chatter, scarcely holding the bridles of the animals, and carelessly allowing them to graze the edge of the precipices. Gradually, however, our actresses gained confidence in these robust mountaineers, who do all the hard work from which the men, devoted solely to war, exempt themselves; but the fatigue was great, for we had to perform in this manner a dozen leagues, almost always bent backward or forward upon our beasts, and unable to breathe except at short intervals upon a level piece of ground. Léon, Marco, and I preferred to walk, but we were obliged to go quickly; the prince, mounted on an excellent horse, which he managed with a dazzling skill, headed the file with two long-mustached attendants running on foot behind him, with carbines on their shoulders and belts furnished with cutlass and pistols. The mountaineers, proud of their strength and courage, made it a point of honor to follow them at a short distance. We followed after, annoyed and embarrassed by our mules and horses, which would not be led along by the bridle, — they were full of ardor and emulation, — but which, always wishing to pass ahead of us, rolled down avalanches of stones upon our legs. Lambesq completely lost his temper with his mule, which, in dodging his blows, lost its head and plunged into the abyss. The prince and his escort did not trouble themselves about it, in the least. We must leave the defile before night, for we were dying of thirst, and the calcareous rock had not the tiniest stream of water to offer us.

At last, in the dusk of the evening, we found ourselves upon the grassy sward of a narrow valley, surrounded on all sides by desolate mountaintops. A great house, surmounted by a dome, with light streaming from its windows, was spread out on a hill at a little distance. It had the appearance of a vast convent. It was a convent in reality. Our prince, although a layman, held the rank of bishop, and this ancient monastery, where his ancestors had reigned as princes, had become the residence wherein he figured as bishop.

I will not explain to you the peculiarities of this social state of a Christian country which is considered Turkish, and which, always at war with its oppressors, really belongs and is subject only to itself. We were on the confines of Herzegovinia and Montenegro. I understood scarcely anything of what I saw there, singular and illogical, according to our ideas. Perhaps I had carried there the carelessness of the Frenchman, and the frivolity of the artist, who travels to encounter new experiences, without caring to penetrate the how and wherefore. To actors, everything is a spectacle; to strolling actors particularly, everything affords surprise and entertainment. If the player fathomed the ideas of others like a philosopher, things would not impress him as he needs to be impressed.

My comrades were like me in this respect. Nothing seemed simpler to them than having a convent for a palace, and a Montenegrine warrior for abbé.

We expected, however, to see a long procession of monks wind under these romantic arches. There was but one, who had charge of the medical and culinary departments. The rest of the Greek community had been transferred to another convent, which the prince had erected at a little distance from the old one. The latter falling in ruins, he had had it repaired and fortified. So it was a citadel, also, and a dozen death's-heads, which adorned the top of one of the turrets, bore witness to the summary justice of the sovereign chief. To cut off heads in the Oriental style, while talking of Déjazet, to fight like one of Homer's heroes, while imitating Grassot, these contrasts sum up for you in two words the indescribable existence of Prince Klémenti.

He had vassals like a baron of the Middle Ages, and these warlike vassals were rather his rulers than his subjects. He was a devoted Christian, and he had a harem of veiled women whom no one ever saw. As with the mixture of manners and customs which characterizes frontier provinces, he had this peculiarity of being French through his mother, and through his collegiate course, he presented the most singular type that I have ever encountered; and I must tell you that, without his comparative wealth and his proved patriotism, he would probably not have been accepted by his neighbors more seriously dramatic, the perpetually insurgent chiefs of Bosnia and Montenegro.

His subjects, to the number of about twelve hundred, were of all origins, and boasted that their ancestors were Bosnians, Croats, Venetians, Servians, Russians; perhaps there had also been *Auvergnals* among them! They were of all religions, Jewish, Armenian, Coptic, Russian, Roman Catholic, Greek Catholic; there was even a considerable number of Mus- sulmans among them, and these lat- ter were none the less devoted to the cause of national independence. The prince likewise possessed a village, that is to say an encampment of idolaters, who, it is said, sacrifice rats and owls to an unknown god.

We were all installed in two chambers, but so vast that we might have engaged in the exercises of the hippodrome in them. Oriental tap- estry, somewhat faded, but still very rich, divided the chamber of the wo- men into several parts, and allowed them each a place of retirement. In that of the men an enormous mat of aloes separated the space into two equal compartments, one for sleep- ing, the other for recreation. As regards beds, there were divans and cushions in abundance, no more sheets or blankets than in the blue room.

The prince, after bidding us good evening, disappeared, and the friar cook brought us coffee and preserved rose-leaves. We thought that this was the custom before a meal, and we expected a supper, which did not come. We attacked the sweetmeats; and, as we were very tired, we con- tented ourselves with them, hoping that the morrow's breakfast would prove a compensation.

At daybreak, feeling very well, notwithstanding, I went to explore the country with Léon. The scenery was charming, an oasis of verdure, in a setting of steep and lofty cliffs, crowned by summits still covered with snow. Through a gap of pecu- liar form, I recognized, or thought I recognized, the peaks of rosy Alps

that we had had leisure to admire in that direction, during our captivity on the rock.

The valley that the manor over- looked was not two *kilomètres* in extent; it was a long savanna, which we crossed rapidly for further ex- plorations. This fine fertile tract, bordered by almond-trees in bloom, seemed enclosed by a calcareous perpendicular wall; but we had no- ticed, in our journey of the previous evening, that the innumerable valleys shut in by the irregular network of these Alps, communicated with each other by narrow openings, and a lit- tle climbing allowed us to penetrate into another valley larger than the first, and well cultivated, which constituted the best portion of the prince's domains. An enchanting little lake within it received the waters issuing from a grotto, and did not return them again to the surface. Léon explained to me that it was a *ponor*, that is to say, one of those numerous streams and subterranean rivers that alternately show and con- ceal their mysterious current, in this almost inaccessible country, whose geography does not yet exist.

This water constituted the wealth of Prince Klémenti; for dryness is the curse of these lands, at the same time that it is the guaranty of their independence. There exist in those regions, I was told, considerable spaces, veritable Saharas, where, for lack of water, hostile troops are un- able to endure a campaign.

On returning from our stroll, we found our actresses making their toilet with soup-tureens and buckets in the kitchen. It had not been supposed that Christians needed to perform ablutions, and the basins and other toilet-vessels of blue English ware which decorated the pantry served to contain game-pies.

Bellamare, on his part, demanded from the monk a more substantial breakfast than the supper of the previous evening. The latter excused himself with obsequious politeness, saying that the repast would be served at noon, and that he had no orders to anticipate it. Again we supported ourselves by patience and much coffee. Brother Ischion, this bearded cook, in black robe and judge's cap, had certainly something else to do than listen to our complaints. He was a sort of Jack-of-all trades, who, at this moment was polishing weapons and horses' bits. As he spoke Italian, he informed us that the prince had departed very early in the morning, to organize a review of his army, which would take place upon the lawn at ten o'clock. He added that probably His Highness intended to offer this entertainment to our most illustrious lordships. We were free to believe this, but in reality the prince had more serious preoccupations.

Our actresses, warned of the approaching solemnity, attired themselves as well as they were able. Their dress-toilets had sustained some serious injuries upon the *Scoglio Maledetto;* but, with the taste and skill of Frenchwomen and *artistes*, they quickly repaired them, and could appear in a style that did us honor. They had the kindness to sew on the buttons missing from our coats, and to iron out more than one shirt-collar outrageously tumbled. At last, by ten o'clock, we were sufficiently presentable, and, after having announced his coming, the prince appeared to us in all the splendor of his military costume ; the white leggings relieved by red and gold lace of marvellous workmanship, the *fustanelle* of snowy white over breeches of scarlet cashmere, the jacket of red cloth loaded with buttons and gorgeous trimmings, with silk sleeves embroidered with gold and silver, the cap, of astrakan and velvet, surmounted by a tuft fastened with precious stones, a belt covered with gold and filled with an arsenal of yataghans and pistols, terminating in heads of birds and serpents. He was so handsome, so handsome, he had the air of having issued from the enchanted box of some genius in the Arabian Nights. He conducted us to the platform of one of the turrets, and it was there that the dissevered heads, which our women had not yet perceived, struck them with horror and disgust. Impéria, to whom the prince had given his arm, and who preceded the others, stifled a cry, and quitting her guide precipitately, sprang upon a winding staircase, calling out to her companions, who followed her : "Not there ! do not go there, it is frightful ! "

The fear of women is always accompanied by an eager curiosity. Although greatly alarmed already, Anna, Lucinde, and Régine wished to see what it was, and returned to us shrieking like mad. The prince began to smile about the corners of his mouth, a little surprised and a little offended ; but he could not persuade them to remain in a place so imbued with the local atmosphere. In vain he told them that Turks' heads were not human heads, and that they were dried by the wind, and consequently quite clean ; they declared that they would forego the pleasure of seeing the review rather than behold it in such company. Klémenti took us to another tower, which vexed him somewhat, as it forced him to modify the programme of his play, that is to say, his plan of drill ; then he left us, and we saw him reappear upon the drawbridge, conspicuous and showy on a magnificent mountain-horse whose every movement betrayed his fiery spirit, and who seemed to wish to devour the others.

The spectacle was very fine. The army consisted of two hundred and fifty men, but what men! They were all tall and muscular, in handsome costumes, armed to the teeth, and admirable horsemen. Their little horses, restive and nervous as Cossack steeds, pawed the ground. They executed several figures in a very skilful manner, imitating cavalry charges especially, descending and reascending the rapid slope of the valley, in the same gallop, leaping enormous ditches, and returning in good drilling order, after a steeple-chase to take one's breath away. Next ensued a little sham-fight among the rocks opposite us. The cavaliers reined in their horses on narrow platforms, and held them with one hand, while they fired their guns with the other ; then, while in full gallop, they practised shooting at Turks' heads, this time artificial.

The prince took part in all these exercises, and displayed a mingled skill and grace which lent new lustre to his enchanting beauty. A Homeric feast next united all the warriors on the greensward. Twenty sheep were served up whole there. Officers and soldiers, seated on the grass, without distinction of rank, ate with their fingers, very gravely and very properly, without soiling their handsome costumes.

The savor of these viands reminded us that we had been almost fasting since Ragusa ; and although they did not seem to think of us, we invited ourselves, and descended from our observatory, with the resolution of people who had no wish to repeat the fast of the accursed rock.

The prince, who presided at the banquet, was preparing to offer a toast which would terminate in a speech. We advanced straight upon Brother Ischion, who was officiating in full blast, and Bellamare caught up a saucepan which boiled on the canteen, and which contained half a sheep with rice. The monk endeavored to prevent him.

" Do you wish me to brain you ? " Moranbois said to him, fixing his hawk's eye upon him.

The unhappy man understood this glance, if not the words of the threat, sighed, and gave up the struggle.

Sheltered and concealed within a clump of lentisk-trees, we passed the time merrily, each of us in turn detaching himself to go out and snatch openly, now a piece of game, now a fish from the lake in the neighboring valley. The prince observed our proceedings, and shaking off the cares of his empire for a moment, slipped among us, excusing himself for not having invited us to this wholly military feast, because it was not the custom to admit strangers to it, and further because the women never ate with the men.

"Monseigneur," answered Bellamare, "we are all *Auvergnats*, neither men nor women, that is to say, all equal. You warriors of the Iliad are free to take us for *Greeks;* but we are hungry, and cannot live on dry preserves. Let us have meat to eat, or send us back; for with the too refined regimen, to which your minister of culinary affairs seems disposed to subject us, we shall never be able to recite three lines for you."

The prince deigned to smile, and promised us that next day we should be treated in the European style.

"You must grant me this day," he added, "devoted to very urgent business. To-morrow I shall be entirely at your service."

"If that is the case," said Moranbois, as soon as his back was turned, "let us supply our pockets for the rest of the day."

And he plunged several roasted partridges into his great travelling-bag.

We went to pass the remainder of the day on the banks of the little lake that Léon and I had discovered in the morning. It was a truly delicious spot. The middle of the water was clear as crystal; but where the subterranean torrent that fed it entered and left the lake it foamed among rocks covered with rose-laurel and blossoming myrtle. We all felt recovered in this oasis, and we abandoned ourselves to a paroxysm of wild gayety, such as we had not known for a long time; even Moranbois and Léon threw off their gravity, and Purpurin attempted to make poetry.

We had a continuation of the spectacle, when we saw, defiling through the path that crossed the plain, these handsome horsemen who had entertained us with their feats, and who now departed in groups, hidden at various turns of the mountain, in pathways which we could not see. From time to time these groups reappeared on dizzy precipices. The gold upon their costumes and their handsome weapons glittered in the setting sun.

"I never went to the opera," said Purpurin, sagely, "but I find that this is even finer."

We were left alone there until evening, when a tall old man with long white mustaches, arms bare to the shoulder, and carrying an enormous gun by way of shepherd's crook, passed by with a flock, paused, and saluting us with a grave and affable air, addressed some remarks to us that none of us understood; but, as he pointed persistently now at the sun, and now at the monastery, we guessed that for some reason we ought to return. It was well we did so, for they were raising the drawbridge when we presented ourselves. The little fortress was rigidly shut up, as soon as the sun sank behind the lowest of the mountains. We were not alarmed at the idea of thus being prisoners every night: none of us foresaw that the thing might become very disagreeable.

Friar Ischion being the only servant who could understand us, we tried to make him talk, when he brought us the excellent Turkish coffee and the eternal sweetmeats, which, according to him, must suffice us after the noonday repast. He informed us that the prince had retained the principal chiefs of his army with him, and was holding council with them in the old hall of the chapter-house.

"Heaven knows," he added, in an emphatic and impressive tone, "what sunbeam or what thunderbolt will result from this conference! peace or war!"

"War with the Turks?" asked Bellamare. "These gentlemen attack them then sometimes?"

"Every year," replied the monk, "and the favorable season is at hand to take some fort or passage from them. Heaven grant that it may not be before two months, for then our lake will be dry! The excellent fish which it supports will have returned into the caverns with it, and the enemy, finding nothing to eat or drink in the country, will not venture to attack us, here in the heart of the mountains."

"What do you live on, then, during the summer?" inquired Régine.

"In the summer," replied the monk, "our gracious master, Prince Klémenti, goes to Trieste or Venice. The rest of us drink sour milk and eat cheese fried in butter, like the other inhabitants of the plain."

"It is not fattening," said Régine, "for one can see the daylight through your ribs."

"It would seem," said Bellamare, when the monk had gone, "that our host means to amuse himself until the time when he enters on his campaign. It was a singular idea to bring us to his house, in the midst of such preoccupations, unless he has enlisted us to form a portion of his army, which is finer than it is large. Say, my children, would it not amuse you to fire your guns at the infidels?"

"Certainly not!" cried Lambesq. "We needed only that! We shall have chanced upon a pretty hornet's-nest!"

"For my part," said Moranbois, who loved, like every one else, to irritate Lambesq, "I should not be sorry to mount the cannon on these little ramparts, and break the heads of some Mahometans."

"Then congratulate yourself," said Léon, continuing the joke; "I know that the prince's intention is to intrust us with the defence of his fortress, when he has entered on his campaign, and ten to one we shall have to sustain some assault."

"I cannot contain myself for joy!" cried Marco; "I have always longed to play genuine melodrama."

The fear and anger of Lambesq restored us to good-humor, and we proposed to pass the evening merrily; but first of all we wished to know if we could make ourselves at home, and be as noisy as we pleased, without annoying our host, and disturbing his council of war. Bellamare, Léon, Marco, Impéria, Lucinde, and I, leading the way with a torch, determined to make a voyage of discovery in this romantic monastery, that we had not yet had leisure to explore. Our apartments opened on a bastion that overlooked another battlemented building, on which a sentinel paced day and night. We could contemplate a fine effect of moonlight streaming through the sharp lines of the fortifications; but in the presence of this sentinel and his regular step there was something troublesome and irritating to us. The scene was not enlivening and the evening was chilly. We decided to seek elsewhere some place suited to our frolics, or to a general *far-niente*, something which might remind us of the greenroom of a large theatre. Passing through long cloisters, with surbased arches, and mysterious staircases which sometimes led only to walled-up doors or to labyrinths of chaos, —for certain portions in the interior of the convent were still ruined,—we discovered the library, which was a very fine apartment, completely stripped of its venerable works, transported, like the printed books, to the new monastery. In one of the closets were a few odd volumes of Eugène Sue and Balzac, with Béranger's poems, besides a book, given as a second prize, at the College Henri IV., to the student Klémenti. A Turkish guitar, deprived of its strings, or rather of its string, for the *guzla* has but one, several long guns, unfit for service, stools to climb on to the empty shelves, rolls of carpet, rickety tables, — in short, a thousand things put by for future use, or worthless rubbish, all bore witness to the entire desertion of this hall, as large as a church, and plentifully lighted by high arched windows; but the moon cast a sepulchral light upon the floor. It needed the illumination of a theatre to brighten up this desert. The women declared that they should die of fear there, and that we must seek some other place.

"Stay!" said Lucinde, "on the highest shelf I see a quantity of wax-tapers, which would procure us an illumination. Try to climb up there, gentlemen."

We assisted Marco to wheel up one of the massive stools, and he had already reached the supply of tapers, when we heard footsteps in the gallery that opened from the back of the library; it was the slow creaking of Friar Ischion's sandals, and each step brought him nearer to us. Like marauding scholars, surprised by the master, we extinguished our light, and all concealed ourselves, some here, some there, behind the divans and the piles of cushions; Marco, crouching on the top of his stool, held himself in readiness to blow out the monk's lamp, if it passed within his reach. We had decided to frighten him rather than allow him to discover our vagabondage; but it was he who froze our blood by the strange scene we were about to witness.

He carried a large basket, which seemed very heavy, and he walked slowly, raising his lamp to guide his way through the confusion of old furniture. When he was quite near us, he paused before the closet which contained the prince's prize and slender library. There, still holding his lamp, and depositing his basket beside him, he drew from it, one by one, the twelve dried heads that we had seen upon the tower;

then, with the hands that prepared the food of his master and his guests, he placed and arranged carefully, one might say lovingly, these hideous trophies on the nearest shelf, after which he regarded them attentively, laid them out again in precise order, as he might have done with a row of dishes on a table, and with his knotty fingers combed the beards still hanging at some chins.

The poor wretch was only acting in obedience to the prince, who, to satisfy our ladies, had ordered him to hide these heads, still preserving them carefully, in his museum ; but the coolness which he displayed in this lugubrious occupation irritated Marco, who, imitating the cry of an owl, threw an armful of tapers at him, and descended precipitately from the stool with the intention of beating him. We restrained him ; the unhappy monk, stretched prostrate on the floor, invoked with a plaintive voice all the saints and gods of the Sclavonic paradise, and strove to exorcise the demons and the wizards. His lamp had fallen from his hands, and was smoking in the folds of his robe. We were thus able to slip off without his seeing us, but imitating, meanwhile, the cries of various animals, each according to his talent, to confirm his belief that he was dealing with spirits of the night.

We no longer had a light, and we groped about in the darkness. I know not when and how we found ourselves in an upper gallery near an archway dimly lighted from below. We saw beneath us, in the obscurity of a sort of chapel, the prince, standing in a little pulpit, opposite a dozen young and old lords or peasants, all equally noble, officers belonging to his corps of partisans ; it was the council of war in the hall of the chapter-house. Klémenti was haranguing them with a clear voice and with a tone of energetic resolution. As we did not understand a word of the Sclavonic language, we could, as from a box in the fourth tier, witness without indiscretion this serious scene, which was not wanting 'in color. I know not if the orator was eloquent. Perhaps he only uttered commonplaces, and doubtless nothing more was needed with people so convinced of their rights, and ' so well disposed to cut off the heads of miscreants ; but his pronunciation was harmonious, and his inflections good enough. When he had finished, we nearly applauded him. Bellamare restrained us and led us quickly away, without their having perceived our presence.

At last we regained our apartment, which was sufficiently remote and isolated to permit us to talk loudly and without constraint. This certainty being the principal object of our expedition, we resolved to take advantage of it. We found a supper served in our great chamber, by Moranbois and Régine, who had spread out their provisions upon a table about a foot high, surrounded by cushions by way of seats, according to the Oriental custom. Anna and Purpurin had likewise been marauding. They had gone into the pantry, and while Ischion was arranging the heads upon the shelf in the library they had stealthily carried off some cakes and several bottles of Greek wine. So the supper was very presentable, and the coffee, Turkish pipes, puns, and songs beguiled the time merrily until three o'clock in the morning.

Nevertheless, I felt inwardly disturbed, in spite of the jests that habit called to my lips. The beauty of the prince and the charm of his peculiar life had, notwithstanding the severed heads, greatly excited the feminine imaginations. The tall Lucinde, the little Anna, even the stout Régine, made no secret of being madly in love with him. The discreet Impéria, when questioned, had replied with the mysterious smile that she always wore on certain occasions.

" I should speak falsely if I told you I did not think this paladin admirable upon his horse. When he dismounts from it, and above all when he speaks French, he loses somewhat. A man like that should speak only the language of fabulous times; but certainly it is not his fault that he is our contemporary. Yesterday I was too tired to look at him. To-day I noticed him; and if he continues to be what he appears, namely, Tasso's Tancred combined with Homer's Ajax, I will agree with these ladies that he is an ideal; but — "

" But what ? " said Bellamare.

" But the beauty that addresses itself to the eyes," she continued, " is only the spell of the moment; the eye of the body is not always that of the soul."

I thought she looked at me, and I felt piqued ; love had revived in me with returning health; I could not

sleep. As Léon was equally wakeful, I asked him, to divert my personal anxiety, if he had noticed Anna's enthusiasm for our host. He answered me in an accent of bitterness that astonished me.

" Why are you angry with me ? " I said to him.

" With you ? " he replied, " I am not ! I am angry with women in general, and the one you have just named in particular. She is the vainest and most feather-headed of all."

" What do you care ? One cannot help laughing. You do not love her; you have never loved her."

" That is a mistake," he answered, in a lower voice ; " I have loved her. Her weakness seemed a grace to me. She was pure, then, and if she had had patience to remain so for some time, I should have committed the immense folly of marrying her. She committed that of yielding too quickly to her absurd infatuations."

" Which is very fortunate for you ; you should be grateful to her."

" No, she rendered me distrustful and misanthropic in the beginning of my career. Shall I make a full confession ? It was for her that I became an actor, as you for — "

" For no one ! what do you mean ? "

" Your prudence and your silence do not deceive me, my friend ! We are both wounded ; you by a love repressed for want of hope, I by a love buried for want of esteem."

It was the only time that Léon opened his heart to me. After that I saw plainly that, if he loved Anna no longer, he would always suffer from having loved her.

The next day Friar Ischion came

to tell us that the prince desired to know at what hour these ladies would be pleased to dine with him. Before replying, we wished to know the customs of His Highness. From the answers of the monk, we gathered that the hero was at the same time temperate and gluttonous. Like wolves, he could fast indefinitely, and, if necessary, eat the earth; but when he sat at table, he ate like four and drank like six. Ordinarily he took but one substantial meal a day, at three o'clock in the afternoon. In the morning and evening he contented himself with trifles. We decided to conform to this programme, on condition that to the trifles should be added eggs, cheese, and plenty of ham for us. All this arranged, we asked the good brother why he was so pale and appeared so languid. He ascribed his fatigue to the enormous repast which he had superintended on the previous day, and carefully refrained from mentioning his hallucination in the library. I ventured to ask him, with an innocent air, why the heads were no longer on the tower. From pale he became livid, made a cabalistic sign in the air, and replied, in a bewildered way, as he left the room, "What the Devil does, God only knows."

"Here," said Bellamare, "is a capital opportunity for us to continue the rôle of the Devil. Let us go and get the heads, and make away with them."

"It is already done," replied Marco, "I would not sleep until I had procured myself some satisfaction. I took a pair of brass tongs, and slipped away to the library. The monk, who had taken to his heels, without waiting for the sequel, had left his lamp extinguished, and his great basket open. I clapped the heads into it, and carried them off."

"And where the deuce have you put them?" cried Régine; "not here, I hope?"

"No! I hid them in a gap of old wall that I closed up with stones. I mean to keep them there until I discover where this old animal roosts. Then I shall adorn his bed with them. I hope that he will die of fright: it is a lesson of propriety that I count on giving him."

"You would do better," observed Moranbois, "to inflict this lesson on the master than on the servant."

"I will think of it," gravely replied the young comedian.

At three o'clock the resonant sound of a frightful rattle announced the dinner, and a servant in livery, whose European costume contrasted with his long mustaches and his warlike expression, informed us by signs that dinner was served. For the first time, Purpurin, recovering his ideas of civilized life, and appreciating things, after his fashion, declared that this Montenegro *Cossack* cut an infernal figure in his ceremonious garb, and that he intended to give him a lesson in good style and good manners. So he hastily donned an old stage livery of the time of Louis XV., put on a powdered peruke, a little paint, and white cotton gloves, and when we entered the refectory he came and planted himself, with a gracious and important air, behind the chair designed for Bellamare. The paroxysm of wild laughter that seized upon us and continued a long time, the agreeable surprise which we experienced at sight of a table, a real table, served in European style, with all the utensils that relieved us from the necessity of tearing the meat with our nails, made us forget that we were very hungry, that the dishes were cooling, and that the prince was making us wait longer than became a man educated in France. At last the door at the back was opened, and there appeared, first a little groom of the most unmistakable Parisian type, in irreproachable English costume, followed by a tall, slender young man attired in a somewhat antiquated French fashion, that is to say, from four to five years behind the prevailing style. He was a handsome fellow, but without grace, and the lower part of his face was injured by an expression of silliness or shyness. We thought that it was a secretary, perhaps a relative of the prince, coming, in his turn, from the College of Henri IV., perhaps a brother, for he resembled him. He spoke, excusing himself for having devoted too much time to a toilet to which he had grown somewhat unaccustomed. O deception! it was the prince himself, looking younger and slighter from the removal of his heavy mustache, shaved, his hair dressed, pomaded, cravatted, his free motions imprisoned in a black coat, the chest confined in a white waistcoat with buttons of fine pearls, and covered with too great a profusion of gold chains; the prince, fallen from the paladin of Ariosto into the Italian dandy, or rather into the *Schiavone*, gotten up as gentleman; numerous specimens of whom we had seen the year before at Venice, where they are insupportable to quiet people from their chattering, their frivolity, and the disturbance that they make in the theatres.

Our Klémenti was more intelligent and better bred than those little lords who go abroad from home in search of civilization, and who do not always bring back its best characteristics. There was in him a chivalric and feudal side which prevented him from being ridiculous; but as the French element transmitted by his mother was deadened in his hard and warlike life, what he strove to reproduce of it was neither of the utmost freshness nor of the first quality. This reverse of the fine medal made us regret the antique profile of the previous evening. The cameo had become a hundred-sou piece.

Deprived of his picturesque costume, he now seemed to us only a third-rate personage. In plumed cap and "fustanelle," he had seemed to speak our language as well as we; dressed like us, the defects of elocution grated on our ears. He had a disagreeable *zézayment*, and used common or pretentious expressions. It was still worse when he wished to imitate our pleasantry. Since his early youth (and he was now thirty-two) he had put by a collection of stale jokes, which had become too hackneyed in the second-class theatres to seem amusing to us. The witticisms that are brought out on the stage are already worn out in the greenroom. Judge how new they must appear when they have passed through two or three hundred performances! The prince, however, was anxious to display them before us, to show us his familiarity with current topics; and instead of talking to us of his romantic country, his combats and adventures, he talked to us of Odry in *Les Saltimbanques*, or of certain opera scandals already out of date and utterly forgotten.

He also essayed to be sprightly, although he was correct and cold as a man who has three wives, that is to say, two too many. He thought to please our actresses; but Régine alone kept him company, and he saw that he had made a blunder in regard to the others. If he frequently lacked taste, he did not lack penetration.

The dinner was plentiful enough to permit us to eat what was eatable. The rest was a senseless mixture of dishes scandalized to find themselves together. Garlic, honey, allspice, curds, assorted themselves as best they could with meats and vegetables. The prince devoured all, indiscriminately. Moranbois, intending an allusion to the banquets of the ancients, remarked in an undertone, that our host had a throat like the antique. The Parisian groom, who was a mischievous monkey, smiled from ear to ear with approbation. The rogue was intensely delighted with the whimsical figure of Purpurin, and, as he served us, played off pranks upon him that cruelly compromised the dignity of our theatrical valet. The other attendants, of whom there were a half-dozen stationed about us, grave and proud in their national costume, were there for

show, and stirred no more than statues. Fortunately, the groom, quick as a lizard, ran about, from one to another, pouring for us floods of a champagne manufactured at Trieste or Vienna or some other place, which would have flown straight to our heads, if it had been good enough to make us lose prudence. Moranbois was not fastidious, but he could drink with impunity; Lambesq still thought himself too ill to run the risk, and Marco, seated beside Léon, was constrained by him to good behavior.

The prince alone warmed up a little, and, the martial instinct reviving in him, he said something, at dessert, about the perpetual struggle of the country against the Turks. A good grain of ambition mingled with his patriotism, and he gave us to understand that he would probably be chosen leader of the permanent insurrection, whose monomania was the unity and independence of the country.

Some one wished to speak to him, and he went out, begging us to await him at the table. Then the groom, who was a stunted fellow of twenty-two, wild with joy at finding some one to talk to, and eager to talk with actors, joined unhesitatingly in our conversation.

"Do not believe," said he, "all that my master tells you. He is a terrible man in battle, I do not deny, but no more so than the others! There are fifty princes like him, who have leagued themselves together to strike a blow at those dogs of Turks, but who all wish to take the chief command. My master will not obtain it; he is too French; his mother was no more noble than I am, and his father was not a direct descendant of the famous Klémentis of old times. They do not look with a favorable eye on the European races that assume to be gentlemen; and this body-guard that you see stuck there like candles, without understanding a word of what we say, despise us; they would like to wring my neck because I shave monsieur when he wishes to make a good appearance for a while."

"If he wishes to appear well, it is to please us, apparently," said Régine; "but say, my little friend, this shaved mustache proves that, for some time, your master does not think of war, for that bluish lip would not be in order."

"It proves, perhaps," replied the groom, "that my lord means to try a bold stroke, without being recognized; one cannot say. It is all the same to me; peace and war are so much alike in this land of brigands, that one cannot tell the difference."

"Brigands!" exclaimed Lucinde; "I have always wished to see them. So there are some near us?"

"It is just so, mademoiselle, and you see some of them there, close by you."

"Come now! Those handsome men!"

"As true as I live! They are like wolves; they do no harm when they are not hungry; but when they want for anything, woe to the people who take a fancy to visit their mountains! They are very peaceable and even hospitable when all goes well with them; but when they are too much molested by the Turks, they have to take from strangers the wherewithal to buy bread and powder. Good people, all the same; only, they are savage and must not be stirred up! There are also bands of robbers who infest the frontier, and call themselves patriots, but of whom it is well to beware. Never walk farther than the little lake, and never venture on the mountain. I tell you this seriously."

This bright and forward young fellow, whose name was Colinet, and whom his master had surnamed Meta (half of a man), would willingly have rambled on, all night, but the prince returned, and carried us off to drink coffee in his drawing-room, which was charmingly appointed, in a very interesting Lower Empire style. He showed us the entire suite of apartments, his sleeping-room, furnished in French fashion, with a French bed, in which he did not sleep, preferring to stretch himself upon a bear-skin in winter, and on a mat in summer, his boudoir, and his study. These rooms were rich, covered with gilding, but destitute of character or real comfort. We preferred to remain in the eastern saloon, where superb chibouques and detestable cigars awaited us; but the thick coffee began to seem delicious to us. We had grown used to it, and the sharp marasquin of the country did not seem so terrible as in the beginning.

The prince drank it until he fell into a torpor much resembling sleep. Impéria took her lace; Régine, perceiving cards, challenged Moranbois to a game of *besigue;* Bellamare invited Léon to play chess; Lambesq took up a number of the *Siècle*, dated three weeks back; and Marco went to sleep, as he always did, when he could not laugh and frolic. The evening threatened to be too peaceful for us, when the prince, sitting up again on his divan, began to recite verses from Racine, pretending to have forgotten them, that he might urge us to declaim them before him.

"This is making us pay our score rather quickly," whispered Bellamare to me; "but as well pay promptly as to run in debt. Let us set about it gayly."

The prince requested a scene from *Phèdre*. This was Lucinde's rôle, but she had been attacked, upon the rock, with a loss of voice, from which she had not wholly recovered, and she was too proud of her fine organ to consent to injure it; she urged Impéria to take her place.

"I have played only Aricie," replied Impéria. "Phèdre is neither within my abilities nor my studies."

"That is no matter," said Bellamare, "you know the part, and, besides, Moranbois is here."

Moranbois had a prodigious memory, and knew by heart all the classic repertory. He concealed himself behind a screen. Impéria and Régine draped themselves in large cashmere shawls that the prince offered them, and placing themselves at a suitable distance, the lights properly arranged, and the royal arm-chair established in state, that is to say, disposed to his liking, they began the scene: —

"Ah! que ne suis-je assise à l'ombre des forêts!"

I was curious to see how Impéria, whose voice was rather crystalline than tragic, would recite these contralto verses, and how her acting, so delicate and careful, would adapt itself to the gloomy attitude of the woman devoured by love. She had laughed beforehand at the *fiasco* she was about to make, and had begged us to applaud her just the same, that the prince, who knew little about it, should not perceive her inadequacy.

What was the surprise, not only of myself, but of Bellamare and all the others, when we saw Impéria suddenly change countenance, and, as if inspired by the idea of her rôle, assume, without ever having studied it, the absorbed and hopeless attitude of the great victim of destiny! Her eye grew fixed and hollow, as if she were still watching, from the accursed rock, the deceitful sails that faded out on the horizon. All that we had suffered came back to us, and a shudder passed through our veins. She felt it vibrate around her, and her face assumed an expression that we did not recognize as hers. Her irreproachable diction gradually accented itself, her cold breast heaved, and her weak voice, grown strident, gained accents of distress, rebellion, and suffocation, which resembled nothing we had hitherto known. Was she feverish? were we delirious? She made us shed genuine tears; and this emotion, doubtless necessary to people who strove to laugh, even amid the terrors of death, wrought us up to an insane excitement. We applauded, we cried, we threw ourselves into each other's arms, we kissed Impéria's hands, and told her that she was sublime. We made more noise

than an entire house. The prince
was forgotten as if he had never
existed.

When I remembered him, I saw
that he was looking at us with astonishment; doubtless he took us
for fools, but it was still a play. He
thought to study the familiar life of
actors, concerning whom people in
the outside world are profoundly
curious, and which he could observe
only at some quite exceptional moment.

The thing interested him. All
that we owed him was not to weary
him. So all was for the best. He had
no need to ask us for another scene;
we all felt a furious desire to play the
tragedy, and to feel ourselves inspired
each by the other. Moranbois, the
Hercules, brought the box of costumes. The prince's boudoir served
as dressing-room for the men, his
study for the women. He remarked
a little stupidly upon the modesty of
our apparel; and Moranbois, who
could not long constrain himself, said
to him, in the most courtly tone he
could command, "Then your Highness had entertained the belief that
we were vulgar people!"

The prince condescended to laugh
heartily at this sally.

In quarter of an hour we had
taken off our swaddling-clothes, and
put on our draperies. I played
Hypolite; Lambesq played Thésée;
Anna, Aricie; Léon, Théramène. We
acted the whole play, I know not
how. We were caught up and lifted
above the earth by the talent that
Impéria had revealed. It seemed
that the shipwreck had changed her
artistic temperament; she was nervous, feverish, sometimes admirable,
always harrowing. She yielded to
the sway of her inspiration; she had
no consciousness of what she did.
She was seized occasionally with a
wish to laugh, which terminated in
sobs. This need of laughter began
to appeal to our nervous systems
also; it was the inevitable reaction
after our tears. When Léon came
to Théramène's recital, of which he
had a horror, he pretended that he
had forgotten it, and Marco, warned
by him, pushed Purpurin, attired in
the most overpowering costume, in
front of Thésée. Purpurin made no
supplication. Delighted to exhibit
his dramatic talent, he began thus,
mingling his two favorite tirades : —

"'A peine nous sortions des portes de Trézène.
C'était pendant l'horreur d'une profonde nuit,
Ma mère Jézabel. . . Ses gardes affligés. . .'"

He could say no more. The
prince rolled over with laughter
upon the cushions, and this was the
signal for an exuberant hilarity on
our part.

While we were taking off our
costumes, Bellamare also enjoyed a
comedy, and it was the prince who
supplied him with it.

"Monsieur Impresario," said this
naïve potentate to him, "you have
kept a secret from me, I know not
why. But at last I discover it, and
you will confess the truth. This
young actress that you call Impéria,
it is an assumed name?"

"All our names are assumed," replied Bellamare, "and this one con-
ceals no mystery worthy to interest
your Highness."

"Pardon me. I perfectly recognized Mademoiselle Rachel."

"Who?" cried Bellamare, beside himself with surprise. "Which one?" "Impéria, I tell you. I have seen Rachel once in this very rôle. It is her height, her age, her voice, her acting. Come, confess it; do not mystify me any longer. It is certainly Rachel, who, to punish me for not having at once recognized her, has forbidden you to betray her incognito."

Bellamare was too honest to lie, and, at the same time, too mischievous to forego the diversion that the prince's singular error promised us. He declared that Impéria was not Rachel, but he declared it with a hesitating accent and an embarrassed air which persuaded our host that he had not been deceived.

When Impéria returned to the saloon, Klémenti kissed her hands respectfully and tenderly, entreating her to keep the cashmere shawl that she brought back to him. She refused it, saying that she had not enough ability and reputation to accept such a gift. Lucinde, who followed her, thought her very foolish, and greatly regretted not having acted Phèdre. Régine said, in an undertone: "Take it; you can give it to me, if you do not care for it."

The prince seemed hurt by the refusal. Bellamare took the shawl, and told the prince that it should be accepted, but dexterously replaced it in His Highness's apartment, rightly thinking that he ought not to make capital of the name of Rachel, and that the present would be acceptable only when it should be offered to Impéria, appreciated for herself.

When we had returned to our own rooms, he regaled us with the anecdote, adding, at the same time, that Impéria had revealed abilities, that evening, which rendered our host's mistake excusable.

"Hush, my friend," replied Impéria, with sudden sadness. "What I have been this evening I appreciate better than you. I indulged in an experiment. I played from impulse, thinking to be detestable, and promising myself to exaggerate still further, if I made you laugh. I made you weep, because you needed to weep; but you will laugh to-morrow, if I repeat it."

"No," said Bellamare, "I am a judge of that; what you chanced upon this evening was truly fine, I give you my word of honor."

"Ah well, if that is true," she replied, "I shall not recover it to-morrow, since I did it unintentionally."

"We shall see!" said Lucinde, who had suffered herself to be led away, like the others, into applauding her companion, but who had had enough of it already, and did not fancy being superseded.

"Let us see directly," replied Bellamare, with the enthusiasm that he was wont to exhibit in his teaching. "I am going to see for myself if it is a fugitive inspiration, such as so many distinguished artists have had at some time in their lives, and which could never be recaptured. Begin again for me here!

  ' Ah que ne suis-je assise —' "

"I am tired," answered Impéria, "it is impossible."

"Tired? an additional reason. Come! try, I wish it; it is for your own sake, my child! try to engrave your inspiration upon the marble, before it has grown cold again. If you regain it, I will note it carefully, and preserve it for you afterwards, so that you shall not lose it again."

Impéria seated herself, endeavored to compose her attitude and face. She recovered neither her expression nor her accent.

"You see plainly," said she, "it was the passing of a breath. Perhaps, even, it was not in me at all. You had the collective hallucination which results from excited imaginations."

"Then it will be like my case," I said to her. "I had the sacred fire on a certain evening, and afterwards — "

"The thing happens to everybody," replied Bellamare. "I remember having played Arnolphe, all one evening, without speaking through my nose. I had quarrelled with my wife that morning, and I was radiant as the stars. Hence, because one falls back into his natural condition, after these prodigies, it does not follow that he can never reproduce and fix them. Never be discouraged, children. Apollo is great, and Bellamare is his prophet!"

The next day Bellamare was summoned by the prince into his study.

"It is necessary," he said to him, "that you perform a courageous act, since you are still somewhat fatigued. I had hoped to allow you some days of rest; but the situation is pressing, and, besides, the presence of Rachel among you — Do not deny; my groom has been talking this morning with your young comedian, who confessed all to him; it is truly Rachel who disguises herself under the name of Impéria. I could not be mistaken in her! I have still the voice of Rachel in my ears, her fine profile before my eyes. If she persists in her incognito, do not contradict her; we will pretend to keep her secret; but the influence of her real name and the spell of her wonderful talent will be of great use to my country. Understand me fully; no one is capable of commanding a great insurrection. All these petty chiefs, equally brave and devoted, are equally lacking in the requisites, — money and intelligence. I am rich myself, and I have received the education that develops a savage into a man. So the general safety is in my hands, if they will but open their eyes. There is a prejudice against me, on account of this very education. They think me a buffoon, because I love the arts. Assist me to win and captivate these uncultured minds. Declaim fine verses to them, of which I will give them a translation of my own making, and whose harmonious solemnity shall strike them with respect. Show them impressive costumes, sing them martial airs. I know that you are all musicians, and lastly, lastly, if Rachel would, if Rachel, appearing again in the style of a few years back, would consent to sing them this *Marseillaise*, which has, they say, stirred up the French people — Come! I know that she does not wish to sing it any more; but here, under a transparent *pseudonyme* — Impéria! *impératrice:* it is so evident! I know well that this song fatigues her greatly; but I have gems to recompense her, and finer cashmeres than the one that she refused yesterday. As for you, Monsieur Impresario, you shall make your own terms, you have not told me your conditions yet; the time has come. Seat yourself at my desk. Write, and I will sign."

Any one but Bellamare, unless a rascal, would have been embarrassed in accepting; but he knew how to combine the honorable man and the man of humor, so he took his resolution on the instant, and wrote as follows : " Prince Klémenti engages for a month the troupe of M. Bellamare, at a thousand francs for each performance that they shall give in the castle of His Highness, with the assistance of Mademoiselle Impéria. There shall be further allowed to the said Mademoiselle Impéria the sum of one thousand francs per representation, if, at the end of the said engagement, Prince Klémenti persists in seeing in her the equal of Mademoiselle Rachel, in the song of the *Marseillaise* and in tragedy ; failing which, there shall be due to the said Impéria only a present, at the option of the said prince."

The prince thought the document ingenious, signed it, and gave a thousand francs in advance. Bellamare, on withdrawing, said to him, to ease his conscience : " I assure Your Highness that Impéria is not Rachel."

" Precisely ! Precisely ! " cried the prince, laughing. " Call your company, and select your theatre. As for me, I am going to issue my invitations for next Sunday."

He summoned Meta, who, having been in his service for three years, had learned the language of the country, and ordered him to serve as interpreter between the company and the workmen that they would have to employ. From that moment Meta, who had taken a violent fancy to us, only left us to dress and shave the prince.

He was a knowing lad, bold and spoiled, a thorough Paris *gamin*, who boasted of having played his part on many a barricade. He had seen Rachel at the free performances, and although he was certain that she was not among us, he had maliciously confirmed the belief of his master, over whom he had the ascendency usually allowed to spoiled children. So he was the principal author of the romance on whose adventures we were about to enter.

Léon greatly blamed the *mezzo termine* of Bellamare, and declared that we were taking a Jesuitical advantage of Rachel's name. Impéria felt considerable unwillingness to be the object of this fraud on the part of the prince toward his invited guests ; but the prince displayed a good faith so obstinate or so well simulated, all our efforts to undeceive him were in vain, that our scruples vanished, and we prepared gayly to play Camille and Racine in the convent-bishop's-palace fortress of Saint Clement.

We could not find a better place than the funereal library. It would contain an audience of four hundred persons,—the maximum specified by the prince, — besides a pretty little stage, with its greenroom, dressing-room, and side-scenes. The solid shelves, which had formerly supported folio manuscripts and volumes printed in every language, were taken down, and rearranged to form a very fine estrade for the spectators. We had workmen in abundance, very active and obedient. They were soldiers of the prince's army. Two monks were brought from the new convent, who, thinking to decorate a chapel, painted for us, in distemper, a very pretty front in the Greco-Byzantine style, and the *harlequin's cloaks*, that is to say, the first stationary side-scenes, which serve as a set-off to the others. An immense carpet performed the office of curtain; it was a little heavy; it took four men to manage it. That did not trouble us. Moranbois undertook the making of the scenery, which he understood better than any one. Léon designed it; I painted it, with the aid of Bellamare and Marco. The back curtain, with a classic peristyle for tragedy, had already been repaired at Gravosa. Lambesq repaired the instruments that had been injured, to the best of his ability. The orchestra, in other words the four of us who supplied their place, were concealed behind the side-scenes, that the actors engaged in the performance might take their part from time to time, without being seen to play the violin or the bass-viol, in the costume of emperor or confidant. Bellamare had introduced an innovation; instead of chorus, at the beginning or end of the acts, a corypheus recited a piece of poetry. These verses, imitated from ancient texts, were very fine; they were by Léon. The orchestra accompanied them noiselessly, with a grave and monotonous rhythm that I had composed, or rather pillaged,

but which produced a very good effect.

While we were thus despatching matters, Impéria studied the *Marseillaise*, which she had never sung in her life, and which she had never heard sung by Rachel; she knew only that, without voice and without musical method, the great *tragédienne* had composed a sort of dramatic melopœia, which was rather mimed and declaimed than sung. Impéria, a musician, could not make so much of the musical theme, and did not hope to attain the sculpturesque beauty, the muffled and terrible accent, of her who had been styled the "Muse of Liberty." Her pure voice had no difficulty in singing, but it was too soft to "arm battalions." She resolved to express herself, according to her nature, whose foundation was calm, resolute, and tenacious. She appealed to her proud and stoical will; she was very simple; she sang quite erect, she looked her audience in the face, with a fascinating fixedness; she advanced upon them, extending her arms, as if she were marching to her death, amid a shower of bullets, with a scornful indifference. This interpretation was a masterpiece of understanding. The first time that she essayed it before us, the first strophe astonished us, the second began to agitate us, the third carried us away. It was not an appeal to enthusiasm; it was like a defiance, so much the more exciting that it was cold and haughty.

"That is it!" said Moranbois, who, you recollect, was the infallible judge of the *effect*, and consequently of the result. "It is not the *Marseillaise* shouted to the people, nor draped for the artists; it is the *Marseillaise* spit in the face of cowards."

We saw the prince only at dinner, during all these preparations. He had much to do, on his part, to invite and reassemble his audience, whose principal members were separated from him by mountains and precipices. All these chiefs of clans were not difficult to lodge. A common hall, rugs, and cushions, they demanded nothing more. They brought all their baggage in their belts, arms, pipes, and tobacco. Not allowing their women to go abroad with them and share their amusements, they greatly simplified the cares of hospitality. This audience without women damped us at first, but it excited Impéria's enthusiasm for the *Marseillaise*.

Lucinde had resumed the part of Phèdre, and, with the exception of the prince and the groom, all the audience seriously took her for the celebrated Rachel. Impéria recited the passages of the corypheus admirably, but they paid no great attention to it. When she appeared at the end, in short tunic, red mantle, and Phrygian cap, bearing a standard with the colors of the local insurrection, they were delighted, and the *Marseillaise* produced the same effect that it had done on us. They listened in silence, then arose a murmur like the first breath of a storm, then a sort of fury broke forth in cries and stamps and threats. A flash passed through the hall, it was the gleam of all the yataghans drawn from their belts and brandished overhead. All these tall, imposing figures, who, since the open-

ing of the play, had regarded us with a majestic and coldly kind attention, became terrible. Their mustaches bristled, their eyes flashed fire, their clenched hands menaced heaven! Impéria was frightened. This audience of desert-lions, who seemed to wish to rush upon her, roaring and showing their claws, made her nearly flee into the greenroom; but Moranbois called to her, with his harsh voice, in the midst of the tumult, "Hold your effect, hold it! always! always!"

She did what she had believed herself incapable of doing: she came forward to the very footlights, braving the spectators, and preserving her dauntless mien, rendered more effective by the delicacy of her figure and her childish face. Then there was a transport of sympathy throughout the hall; all these heroes of the *Iliad*, as Bellamare called them, kissed their hands to her in their simple way, and threw her their scarfs of silk and gold, their chains of gold and silver, even to the rich clasps on their caps: it took an hour to gather them all up.

The prince had disappeared during this uproar. Where was he? Very open with us, but very wily with his countrymen, he had received his guests in French costume, delighting to irritate them by this affectation, and wishing to force them to accept him as a half-breed who was worth all their pure descent. In the interval that the long and noisy triumph of Impéria afforded him he had hastily assumed his most magnificent state costume, and had replaced his fine parade mustache, which was at all times artificial, his own being naturally slight. He thus appeared upon the stage, and presented the pretended Rachel with an enormous bouquet of mountain anemones and myrtle-blossoms, whose stems were fastened with a bracelet of diamonds.

He accompanied this offering with a speech, in the language of the country, which he uttered with his face turned toward the audience, and which expressed the ardent patriotism and the implacable national *vendetta* that the genius of the actress had made to vibrate and quiver through these heroic souls. Then, seeing that his hearers hesitated to accept these facile transformations of his person, the prince added some words, touching his jacket and his beard, and striking his hand upon his heart. That was easy to understand. He told them that the worth of a man was not in a dress that he could procure for money, nor in a mustache that the barber could replace as well as take away, but that it was in a valiant heart that God alone could put within his breast. He accented this last touch so well, and his gesture was so energetic, that he forced his effect like a masterly actor who fires the house. He had certainly studied Lambesq, and spoke quite as well as he in his dialect. We gave the signal for applause, behind the curtain, and the excited audience gave him the ovation that he had designed.

Impéria, returned to the green-room, fainted from fatigue or emotion. On regaining her consciousness, she saw at her feet the heap of offerings that had been thrown to her. She made Moranbois take them away, as belonging to the association, and, in spite of anything that we could say, we had to put them in the common fund. She kept only two handsome scarfs, which she gave to Lucinde and Régine, who were only *pensionnaires*. Bellamare insisted, however, that she should retain the diamond bracelet, in order to wear it before the prince, who did not understand refusals, and attributed them only to a scorn for the value of the proffered article.

We played the tragedy, like this, four times in one month, before an audience each time more numerous, and still the *Marseillaise* excited the same enthusiasm and made a shower of gifts rain down upon the stage. It was like our experience at Toulon, only the presents were more costly; and, as the prince persisted in wishing to persuade the others and himself that no one but Rachel was capable of singing the *Marseillaise* as Impéria sang it, we saw ourselves in possession of a fine sum, and of a property convertible into cash, such as ancient jewels and brocaded tissues, knives, pipes, and other rich and curious objects. Impéria was very seriously offended when we sought to separate her interests from ours. She insisted that the association compact should be executed to the letter. She profited by her donations, only to give some handsome present to the *pensionnaires*. Lambesq was not passed over, in spite of his misconduct. He had roared verses with cyclopean vibrations that had produced more effect than the correct and studied acting of Léon. So he had contributed to our success, and we owed him some reward. He had not expected it, and showed himself very grateful.

Success is life to an actor: it is security for the present, it is boundless hope, it is confidence in the lucky star. We were united as brothers and sisters; no more jealousy, no more pique, no more ill-humor; a perfect kindness towards each other, an inexhaustible gayety, a health of iron. We had that wonderful exuberance of vitality, and that childish improvidence, that characterize the profession when all goes well. We pursued our studies ardently, we introduced improvements in our *mise-en-scène*. Bellamare, having no outside cares, devoted all his time to us, and caused us to make real progress. Léon was no longer gloomy. The pleasure of hearing his poetry well spoken by Impéria restored him to a mood for inspiration. We led a charming life in our oasis. The weather was superb, and allowed us frequent strolls through a country interspersed with splendid horrors and hidden wonders. We did not perceive the shadow of a brigand. It is true that when we ventured out a little in the mountains, the prince furnished us with an escort; at such times we went on hunting expeditions, and the women rejoined us with provisions, for luncheon, in the wildest spots. We had a passion for exploring, and no one suffered any longer from low spirits.

The inhabitants of the valley had conceived a friendship for us, and offered us a touching hospitality. They were the most honest, the gentlest people in the world. In the evening, when we went back to the fortress, it seemed as if we were returning home, and the grating of the drawbridge behind us produced no disagreeable impression on us. We prolonged our studies, literary dissertations, merry quips, laughter, and jests, very far into the night. We were never exhausted, never weary.

The prince was often absent, and always unexpectedly. Was he preparing for a bold stroke, or was he stirring up his party, to obtain the chief command? Meta, who chattered more concerning his affairs than we inquired, pretended that there were great intrigues for and against his master, that there was a most formidable competitor named Danilo Niégosh, who had more chance of success in the province of Montegro, where Klémenti would certainly fail, despite his efforts, his outlays, his entertainments, and his theatre.

"There is only one thing," said he, " that could make him succeed; it would be to take from the Turks, with only his own troops, some important fortification. These gentlemen, when they act all together, perform equal feats; so the ambitious ones naturally wish to do some brilliant deed, without warning anybody, or to succeed with their little band in an enterprise that the others would have considered impossible. In that way they sometimes do astonishing things; but so it is, also, that they very often overdo it, are attacked and outnumbered, and so there is no end to it."

The groom was, perhaps, right; still, we could not help admiring these handsome chiefs, barbarous in manners and customs, but proud and indomitable, who chose rather to live like savages in their mountain fastnesses than to abandon them to the enemy and abide in civilized countries. We felt more respect and sympathy for them than for our prince, and it seemed to us that the other leaders had no reason to envy him his literature and his borrowed beard. We thought ourselves absurd to wish to infuse into them a civilization of which they had no need, and which had only served to make the prince less poetical by half.

Perhaps you will think us in the wrong, and that we reasoned too much like artists; it may be. The artist is charmed with the local atmosphere, and does not heed the obstacles that it presents to progress. I have told you that he does not go to the bottom of ideas; he is full of fancies, he is made up of imagination and sentiment.

We did not argue with the prince. It would have been very useless, and he gave us no opportunity. When he came to our rehearsals, or when he took us into his Byzantine saloon, he squeezed us like lemons to express our wit and gayety for his entertainment. Had he a real desire to amuse himself and forget his petty fever of ambition with us, or did he exert himself to play the part of a frivolous man with us, to lull the suspicions of certain rivals?

Whatever might have been his intention, he was perfectly social and agreeable, and we could not refuse to be social with him. He certainly made us pay our bill at his table, and earn the money of our compact, for he very often asked a performance *gratis*, for himself alone, and he was convulsed with laughter before the excellent comedy of Bellamare and the easy burlesque of Marco; but he showed himself neither distrustful nor penurious, and we did not wish to be in arrears with him. If he had not always an excellent style, he had, at least, the wit to overwhelm our actresses with consideration and attentions, without making love · to any of them. As Anna continued to have a strong infatuation for him, we had feared a little awkwardness in this connection. We did not play the pedagogue with these ladies, but we detested people who came to bill and coo before the actors' faces, and thereby force them to play the jealous or the complaisant rôle, even when they may be neither the one nor the other. In the provinces and in a small company, the situation is sometimes insupportable, and we were no more ready to submit to it in an Oriental palace than in the greenroom of Quimper Corentin. Anna had received fair warning that, if the prince threw her the handkerchief, we would be neither confidants nor witnesses.

The prince was shrewder than to conceal his love-affairs. He abstained from all gallantry. He desired that we should be well, and in full possession of our abilities; he did not wish to make trouble among us, and we were grateful to him for it. We owed him a month of unclouded happiness. I need to recall it, that I may speak of him with justice to you. How little we foresaw by what a horrible tragedy we should pay for his splendid hospitality!

I must, however, arrive at that distracting event, that atrocious scene, whose memory always covers me with a cold perspiration to the very roots of my hair.

We had fulfilled our engagement. We had played *Phèdre*, *Athalie*, *Polyeucte*, and *Cinna*. The prince had kept his promises, and made us rich. When arranging with us, he showed us a letter from Constantinople, in which he was informed that Zamorine had gone to Russia. This rascally adventurer had given us the slip; we were under no obligations to him. He left us to pay the expenses of our recent voyage, but we were too well recompensed to complain, and Bellamare was undecided whether to go to Constantinople on our own account, or to return to France by way of Germany. The prince was in favor of the latter plan. Turkey would afford us only deceptions, dangers, and destitution. He urged us to proceed to Belgrade and to Pesth, predicting a great success in Hungary; but he begged us to come to no decision before a short absence which he was obliged to make. Perhaps he would ask another fortnight of us, under the same conditions. We promised to wait for him three days, and he departed, once more urging us to consider his house as our own. He had never shown himself more friendly. He persisted so resolutely in taking Impéria for

Rachel, that he said to her on bidding her adieu: "I hope that you will not carry away an unpleasant impression of my uncivilized country, and that you will say a little good of me to your generals and your ministers."

So we remained very tranquil under the protection of twelve garrison soldiers, who did duty in the house and in the fortress, alternately domestics and soldiers. I have told you they were grave, handsome men, who did not understand a word of French. A sort of lieutenant, named *Nikanor* (I shall never forget it), and who commanded in the absence of the prince, spoke Italian very well, but he never spoke to us. We had nothing to do with him; his duties were wholly military. He was a tall old man, whose sinister glance and thin lip did not please us. We fancied, not without reason, that he had a profound scorn, perhaps a secret aversion, for us.

Our immediate attendance was performed by Friar Ischion and little Meta, and as far as possible we dispensed with their service. The monk was dirty, curious, obsequious, and false. The groom was a chatterbox, familiar, but a stupid rascal, said Moranbois.

It was not, then, without displeasure that we saw our little Marco establish an intimacy with this young fellow, even to the point of thee-ing and thou-ing each other, and separate himself from us more and more to go about the cloisters and the offices with him. Marco replied to our reproofs that his father was a workman of Rouen, as Meta's father was a Paris workman, that they had spoken the same slang from childhood, that Meta had quite as much wit as he; in short, that they were entirely on a par. He gave as pretext for his eternal marauding with this Frontin, the pleasure of enraging the monk, who was an old pest, and detested both of them. It was easy to see that the monk held them in utter horror, although he never complained of their misdeeds, and appeared to endure them with angelic patience. The incident of the Turks' heads still lingered in his memory. He had found them again, upon the altar of a little oratory where he performed his devotions and jammed his preserves. He had very readily surmised the author of this profanation. I do not know if he had complained of it to the prince. The prince had seemed entirely ignorant, and the heads had never reappeared.

As our table was now as well served as the resources of the country and the culinary skill of Ischion permitted, we had formally forbidden Marco and Meta to steal anything from the pantry; and if they continued this plunder, it was on their own account, and without our knowledge.

One day they came to the rehearsal with faces of extreme confusion, laughing in a singular manner, rather nervous than merry. We did not like to have Meta in our way, during these exercises. He disarranged and handled everything, and did nothing but chatter. Bellamare, annoyed, dismissed him somewhat harshly, and reproved Marco, who had been tardy and rehearsed every-

thing wrong. As this did not often happen to him, and as he was really in fault, we thought we ought to let Bellamare's lesson produce its impression on him, and did not seek to effect an immediate reconciliation between them. After the performance he disappeared. We never forgave ourselves this severity, and Bellamare, so sparing of reprimands and so fatherly with the younger artists, reproached himself for it as for a crime.

We still dined at three o'clock, in the great refectory. Neither Marco nor Meta made their appearance. We thought that they were sulking, like children as they were.

"How foolish they are!" said Bellamare; "I had already forgotten their misdeeds."

Evening came, and the collation was served to us by Ischion in person. We asked him where the two boys were. He replied that he had seen them go out with lines to fish in the lake; that doubtless they had returned too late, and had found the drawbridge raised, but that there was no reason for anxiety about them. Everywhere in the village they would find people ready to afford them hospitality until the next day.

The thing was so probable, we had been so well received every time that we had passed through the village, that we felt no uneasiness. Nevertheless, we were struck by what Lambesq told us, on returning to our room. He asked us if we knew that the prince had a harem.

"Not a harem, exactly," replied Léon; "it is, I believe, what they call an *odalik*. He is not, like the Turks, married to one of his women, and possessor of the others by acquisition. He has simply several mistresses, who are free to leave him, but who have no desire to do so, because they would be sold to the Turks. They live in perfect harmony, probably because it is the custom among Eastern women, and they keep themselves concealed, because that is the manner of loving, or the point of honor, among the men.

"It is possible," responded Lambesq ; "but do you know within what corner of this mysterious mansion they are immured ? "

"Immured ?" said Bellamare.

"Yes, immured, really immured. All the doors communicating with the portion of the convent that they inhabit have been walled up; it is the former laundry, where there is a very fine cistern. They have converted this laundry into a very luxurious bathing-room ; they have planted a little garden in the yard ; they have built a very pretty kiosk, and these three ladies live there without ever going out. They have a negress to attend them, and two sentinels to guard the only door of their prison, which is reached by a passage contrived in the thickness of the walls. This precious prince has the modest freedom of the Orientals."

"How do you know these particulars ?" asked Bellamare, with surprise. "Have you had the imprudence to prowl around there ?"

"No ; that would be bad taste," replied Lambesq, and Heaven knows if these ladies are houris or frights ! In short, I have not been tempted ; but that little piece of impudence, the groom, found the key of the mysterious passage in the prince's apartment, and he has used it several times, in order to see, without being perceived, these ladies at their bath."

"He told you that ? "

"No; it is Marco who told me, and even — "

"And even what ?"

"I don't know that I ought to tell you ; he confided it to me one evening when he was tipsy, and made up with me more than was necessary. I could very well have dispensed with his confidences ; but I confess I was curious to see if he was making sport of me, and he gave me details that convinced me. In short, I believe it is well that you should know it ; Meta has taken him with him to see the toilet of the odalisques, and it has turned his head. I wager that he was there yesterday, when we waited for him, at rehearsal, and perhaps the thing is not without danger for him. I know not how the prince's *icoglans* would take the pleasantry, if they detected him in his curiosity."

"Bah ! we are not among the Turks," replied Bellamare, " they would not impale him for it; but the prince would be extremely displeased, I suppose, and I shall severely oppose these escapades. Marco is a good and worthy lad , when he understands that these little follies would tarnish our honor, he will renounce them. You have done well, Lambesq, to tell me the truth, and I regret that you did not tell me sooner."

We went to bed tranquilly, but some vague presentiment disturbed my sleep, and I awoke before day-break. I thought of Marco, in spite of myself; I could have wished that he had returned.

It had thundered in the night, and the apartments were oppressive with a dull heat. Feeling affected by it, I did not wish to awake my companions; I passed out noiselessly upon the terrace that overlooked a neighboring bastion, and whence could be seen, a little farther off, the entrance tower, outlining itself against a sky covered with clouds. The greenish morning light brought out the irregular forms of this thick, moveless vapor. The fortress, thus viewed, looked like a pile of black masses, solemnly gloomy.

There were, it seemed to me, some persons on the tower, but they did not stir. I thought it was a group of storks asleep upon the battlements. Day advanced, however, and soon it was impossible for me not to recognize the Turks' heads, replaced triumphantly upon their iron rods. It was doubtless an infringement upon the orders of the absent prince, for it could not be his intention to offer this challenge to the nervous susceptibility of our actresses; but it was a defiance from his people, perhaps a menace addressed to us. I went and cautiously awakened Bellamare, to acquaint him with this circumstance. While he was dressing to go out with me, in order to satisfy himself of it, the last vestiges of night had fled, and we distinctly saw, between two battlements that faced us, Marco and Meta, who were looking at us.

"Then they have made them pris-oners," said Bellamare to me, "and have forced them to pass the night in company with those cut-off heads, to punish them — "

The words died upon his lips; each instant increased the intensity of the morning sunshine. The two youths were motionless, as if they had been tightly chained, their chins leaned on the border of the platform. They had a livid pallor; a frightful grin contracted their half-open mouths; they regarded us with a fixed gaze. Our gestures and our calls produced no impression on them; some drops of blood oozed over the stone —

"They are dead!" cried Bellamare, clasping me in his trembling hands. "They have executed them. Those are only their heads!"

I almost fainted, and, for some moments, I knew not where I was. Bellamare, also, fell back and staggered like a drunken man. At last he summoned up his self-command.

"We must know," he said; "we must chastise— Come!"

We aroused our comrades.

"Listen," Bellamare said to them, "there is something atrocious, an infamous murder — Marco and Meta! — Hush! not a word, not a cry — Think of our poor women who have already suffered so much!"

He went to fasten their door on the outside, and gave the key to Léon, saying: "You are not strong, you could not aid us. I confide the women to you; if they come to trouble them, strike on our tam-tam, we shall hear you, we do not leave the house. Say nothing to them, if they do not wake before the accustomed hour, and if they do not try to go out. From their chamber they cannot see this horrible thing. Come, Moranbois! come, Lawrence! You two are equal to ten men in point of muscle; I, too, am strong when it is necessary. And you, Lambesq, listen! you are very muscular also; but you did not love Marco. Are you generous enough, good comrade enough, to be willing to avenge him, even at the risk of your own life?"

"You doubt it?" answered Lambesq, with an accent of courage and sincerity that he had never had upon the stage.

"It is well!" responded Bellamare, pressing his hands with energy. "Let us take weapons, daggers especially; we have plenty of them here."

Moranbois opened the box, and in the twinkling of an eye we were equipped. We repaired to the entrance-tower. It was unguarded; no one seemed to have risen in that part of the fortress; the bridge was not yet lowered. The sentinel, who watched the neighboring bastion, alone regarded us with an indifferent glance, and did not interrupt his monotonous pacings for a moment. His orders had not foreseen our design.

First of all we wished to assure ourselves of the truth, evident as it was. We ascended the winding staircase of the tower, and found there only the bloody heads of the two unhappy boys. They had been severed at a blow, by the Damascus blades that the Orientals use so cruelly well; their bodies were not there.

"Let us leave the heads where they are," said Bellamare to Moranbois, whose teeth chattered with grief and anger. "The prince returns to-day; it is necessary that he should see them." .

"Ah well, he shall see them," replied Moranbois; "but I will not have these innocents remain in the company of this Turkish carrion."

And, as if he had needed to vent his wrath, he tore the dried heads from their supports, and flung them on the paved floor of the court-yard, where their skulls broke with a sharp crash.

"That is useless!" Bellamare said to him.

But he could not prevent him, and we left the tower, after covering those two unhappy faces with our handkerchiefs, as we would not leave them to form a spectacle for the derision of their executioners. We took the key of the tower, and, as we were leaving it, we saw that, although the sun had risen, the bridge was still drawn up, contrary to custom; they had made us prisoners.

"It is all one to us," said Moranbois; "it is not outside that we have business."

There were two guards stationed under the portcullis. Bellamare questioned them. Their orders forbade them to reply; they had the air of not hearing. At this moment the Friar Ischion appeared on the other side of the moat. He carried a basket filled with eggs, which he was bringing from the village. Then he had been up early enough to know what had occurred during the evening or the night. Bellamare waited until he had been admitted, and, as Moranbois shook him roughly in order to make him speak more quickly, we had to defend him; he was the only one who could understand and answer us.

"Who has assassinated our comrade and the prince's groom?" said Bellamare to the terror-stricken monk. "You know it; come, do not affect surprise."

"In the name of the great Saint George," replied the monk, "do not break my eggs, Excellency! They are all fresh; it is for your breakfast."

"I will crush you like a viper," said Moranbois, "if you pretend not to hear. Is it you who have murdered these children? No, you would not have had the courage; but it is you who have spied upon them, accused them, delivered them up. I am sure of it, and I give you my word that you shall not carry your foul head into paradise."

The monk fell upon his knees, swearing by all the saints of the Greek calendar that he knew nothing, and that he was innocent of any evil intention. He evidently lied; but the two guards, who had been tranquilly looking on, began to grow somewhat excited, and Bellamare did not wish that they should interfere, before we had obtained an answer from the monk. He made him declare that the only authority who could be responsible for an execution in the fortress was the commandant, Nikanor.

"And what other would have power over the people?" replied the monk. "In the absence of the prince, there must be a master here, of course; the commandant has right of life and death over all the inhabitants of the fortress and the village."

"Over you, dogs of slaves, it may be," said Moranbois; "but over us, that is what we will see! Where is he burrowed, your beast of a commandant? Show us to his kennel, and do not argue!"

The monk obeyed, bewailing, meanwhile, his eggs, broken by the rough movements of Moranbois, and laughing in his sleeve at our indignation. He led us to the tiger's den; no doubt he hoped we should not leave it.

II.

At the end of the second court, in an arched hall, low and sombre, we found the commandant couched upon a mat, and smoking his long *chibouque* with peaceful majesty. He was not guarded in the least. Considering us vile mountebanks, it had not entered his mind that we could call him to account.

"Is it you who have assassinated our companion?" Bellamare said to him in Italian.

"I have never assassinated any one," replied the old man, with an imposing calmness which staggered us for an instant. And, without quitting his careless attitude, he drew a whiff from his pipe, and looked another way.

"Do not play upon words," replied Bellamare. "It is by your order that they have butchered the two boys?"

"Yes," answered Nikanor, with the same coolness, "it is by my order. If you are not satisfied, appeal to the prince, and if he blame me, I shall have deserved it; but I have no account to render to any one but him. Be prudent, and leave me in peace."

"We are not here to respect your repose," replied Bellamare. "We question you; you must answer, whether you like it or not. Why have you condemned these unfortunates?"

Nikanor hesitated a moment, then, emphasizing the pretentious slowness with which he spoke Italian, he answered: "It is for a personal offence against the prince."

"What offence?"

"The prince alone will know it."

"We wish to know it, and we will know it!" cried Moranbois with his hoarse voice, which became terrible.

And in the twinkling of an eye, seizing Nikanor by the beard, he had thrown him, face downward, on the floor, and set his knee upon his neck.

The old man thought that his hour was come; he had not deigned to think of defending himself; he said to himself, doubtless, that it was too late, and that he was about to endure the pain of retaliation; he remained silent, and gave no sign of hope or fear.

"I forbid you to kill him," said Bellamare to Moranbois, who was literally beside himself. "I wish him to confess."

He made a sign to us; we closed the gate behind us, thrusting the heavy staple into a very primitive fastening. The monk had followed us, through curiosity or to summon assistance, if it should be necessary.

Lambesq, catching sight of the cords and gags that were always there, bound and gagged him quickly. We had deprived the commandant of his weapons; and as there was a sort of rack there containing a half-dozen long garrison muskets, we were in condition to sustain a siege.

"Now," said Bellamare, who had raised Nikanor again, and was holding a pistol to his throat, "you will speak!"

"Never," responded the inflexible mountaineer, without varying his cold and haughty accent.

"I will kill you!" said Moranbois to him.

"Kill," replied he; "I am ready."

What could we do? We were disarmed by this stoical indifference to life. Besides, the vengeance was too easy.

"You will at least tell us," said Moranbois, "the name of the executioner?"

"There was no executioner. I myself have slain the culprits, with the sabre that you hold. If you use it against me, you will commit a crime. As for me, I have done my duty."

"I will not kill you," replied Moranbois, "but I would like to beat you like a dog, and I will beat you. Put yourself on the defensive, you are the strongest man in the country. I have seen you in the exercises of the drill. Come, defend yourself. I mean to knock you down, and spit in your face. Only, not a cry, not a signal to your men, or I will blow your brains out for a coward."

Nikanor accepted the challenge with a scornful smile. Moranbois seized him by the waist; they remained, for a moment, locked in each other's grasp, and as if petrified in the tension of their muscles; but, at the end of this brief instant, Nikanor was once more under the feet of the Hercules, who spat in his face, and cut off his mustache with the Damascus sabre which had severed the head of Marco.

We stood by, motionless, and watched this chastisement. The blood of our comrade came between us and any sentiment of pity; but we could not kill a disarmed enemy, and we were prepared to prevent Moranbois from becoming intoxicated with his own anger. Suddenly we were enveloped in a cloud of smoke, and musket-balls, fired from the window of the ground-floor, whistled about us. By some miracle they hit only the unhappy monk, who had an arm broken. Before the soldiers who came to the aid of their leader could repeat the attack, we had thrust before the long and narrow window the long and narrow divan of the captain. We were besieged, and we were delighted to have something to do. They battered the door, but it resisted. The lifeless commandant moved no longer; the monk writhed in vain. You may well believe that none of us thought of him. We cautiously made an opening between the divan and the window, and we discharged a volley that scattered the enemy; but they returned; we had to close up afresh and repeat our fire. I believe that they had a man wounded. They judged that we were impregnable on that side, and reunited all their efforts against the door,

which yielded, but which Moranbois held in such a manner as to allow passage to only one man at a time. Bellamare seized the first that presented himself; he grasped him by the neck and threw him down; the others, rushing precipitately in, almost suffocated him by walking over his body. I caught the second. It was easy for us to seize the barrel of their guns as soon as they appeared, to divert their aim and lay hold of the man. This hand-to-hand struggle was totally unlooked for by them. They did not think us capable of thus resisting. They had not formed the least idea of the force of that spontaneous spring which makes the Frenchman invincible at a given moment. They were nine against our four, but we had the advantage in position. Now they were ten, now twelve; they were all there, but three or four were disabled, and the others recoiled. They took us for demons.

They returned; they thought that we had killed their leader; they meant to avenge him, though they perished one by one. Truly, they were brave, and, while felling them, we could not make up our minds to kill them. We might have done it. They were hardly in our grasp before their faces expressed, not fear, but stupor, a certain superstitious horror; succeeded quite as suddenly by the resignation of fatalism to a death that they believed inevitable. We left them stretched upon the ground, and they lay perfectly still, fearing lest they might seem to ask for quarter.

I know not how long this mad struggle lasted. None of us felt conscious of it. As far as I could gather, from some words of their language that I had learned, they said that we were sorcerers, and spoke of bringing straw to smoke us out; but they had not time. An exclamation from without and the sound of a well-known voice stopped the combat and ended the siege. The prince had arrived. He imposed silence on them, made them throw down their arms, and advanced toward us, crying, " It is I ! What is the matter ? Explain yourselves ! "

We were too much out of breath to answer. Streaming with sweat, black with powder, our eyes starting from our heads, we were all stammering.

Bellamare, who had fought like a lion, was the first to recover himself, and, imposing silence on Moranbois, who wished to speak, he led the prince to the commandant, who had regained consciousness, as if the unexpected apparition of his master had called him back to life and to his orders.

" Monseigneur," said Bellamare, " with his own hand this man has cut off the heads of our comrade Marco and your servant Meta, two Frenchmen, two boys, for a fault, perhaps a frolic, that he would not tell us, and that he has sworn to tell to no one but yourself. We were mad, we were drunk, we were enraged, and still only one of us challenged him, knocked him down, and cut off his mustache, — spitting in his face, I must and will tell you all ; if he is not satisfied, we are ready to fight a duel with him, all of us, one after another. That is all the revenge that we have taken on him; and, if

you do not think it mild, you ask too much of Frenchmen who have a horror of cowardly ferocity, and who regard the murderer in cold blood as an infamous monster. Your soldiers came to the assistance of their chief; I do not say that they were wrong. They wounded your cook in the endeavor to kill us. We had no hand in it, he will tell you so himself. We could have killed our prisoners, and we have not even struck them with our weapons, but have fought with fists and arms. If they smart for it, so much the worse for them ! You do not find us disposed to repentance, and we will all perish before saying that your customs are humane, and that the acts of severity committed in your name are just. There, I have said."

" And we support you," added Moranbois, drawing down his fur cap over his head.

The prince had listened without manifesting the least surprise, the least emotion. He was in the presence of his escort and of Nikanor, who listened impassible and silent likewise. He was acting his rôle of superior man ; but he was pale, and his eye seemed to seek a solution that might satisfy the pride of his barbarians and the exigencies of our civilization.

He remained wrapped for a moment in this silent meditation, before replying; then he gave some rapid orders in the Sclavonic language. The monk was removed directly, and a glass of brandy poured out for Nikanor, who could hardly stand, and whom the prince would not permit to sit before him ; then everybody left us, and the prince, addressing the commandant, said to him in Italian with a cold, harsh tone : " Have you killed Meta and Marco ? Answer in the language that I use to question you."

" I have killed them," responded Nikanor.

" Why have you done this ? "

Nikanor replied in Sclavonic.

" I have ordered you," returned the prince, " to answer in Italian."

" Shall I tell this thing before strangers ? " replied the mountaineer, with some excitement and almost reddening.

" You will tell it ; I wish it."

" Ah well, master, the valet and the actor saw your women at their bath."

" Is this all ? " said the prince, coldly.

" It is all."

" And you killed them in your anger, on taking them in the act ? "

" No, I was warned that it had continued for several days. I watched for them and seized them in the passage from your apartment, yesterday, at two o'clock in the afternoon. I led them noiselessly to the dungeon, and this night, in presence of your women, I cut off their heads, which are now upon the tower. No other man, except the monk, has known the cause of their death. Your honor has received no stain ; I have done what you ordered, what every man ought to do, or command his servant, or expect from his friend."

The prince turned pale. He could no longer conceal from us the similarity of his Christian customs to the manners of the Turks, and he was deeply mortified. He attempted, however, to justify himself in our eyes.

" Monsieur Bellamare," he said in French, " if you were married, and an impudent libertine came to peep through a door at your wife, when undressed, would you pardon him this outrage ? "

" No," said Bellamare. " My first movement would probably be to throw him out of the window, or to precipitate him down stairs head-foremost ; but I should do it myself, and, if I had to deal with two boys, I should content myself with kicking them out. In any case, had I been even more outraged, I should charge none of my friends to cut off my rival's head in cool blood, and to plant it triumphantly on the roof of my house."

The prince bit his lip, and turned to Nikanor.

" You have never understood your orders," he said to him ; " and, like a brute as you are, you have interpreted in the Turkish style the laws and customs of our nation. It is penalty of death for those who penetrate into our gynecœum, and who establish guilty relations with our women ; but here the case was different ; you surprised no one in my gynecœum, and you have punished, with the extreme rigor of the law, two foreigners, not subject to our authority, and guilty only toward their own honor. Go, put yourself under arrest, until your punishment is decided."

He added in a firm tone, " Justice shall be done."

But I fancied I intercepted a

meaning glance which said to the commandant : "Be easy, you shall be let off with several days' imprisonment."

Whatever it might be, we could demand nothing more, and no satisfaction to our dignity could restore to life our poor little comrade. We only asked of the prince, with a sufficiently cold manner, that his remains should be returned to us, in order that they might be decently interred.

"It is too just," replied he, evidently annoyed and disconcerted by this demand ; "but I cannot permit the burial to take place openly ; wait until night."

"And why then ?" said Moranbois, indignant. "An infamous deed has been committed among you, and you are unwilling that the reparation should be open! It is all the same to us ; we need no one to bury our dead ; but we desire the body of our poor boy, we desire it at once, and if they conceal it from us we will search everywhere for it ; and if they try to hinder us from guarding it against outrages — Ah well, when we are rested, we will begin again to worry your janizaries."

The prince pretended not to hear this harangue, the last word of which, comparing him to a sultan, must have vexed him greatly. He walked up and down the hall of the bodyguard, with a preoccupied air.

"Pardon," he said, as if emerging from a profound revery.

And addressing himself to Bellamare, "What do you ask of me?"

"The corpse of our comrade," replied Bellamare. "Your Highness will dispose of that of your unhappy servant as you think best."

"Poor boy !" said the prince with a deep sigh, real or affected.

And he went out, telling us to wait a moment. He did not return ; but, at the end of ten minutes two men belonging to his escort brought us the mutilated body of the unhappy Marco rolled in a mat. Moranbois took it in his arms, and, while he was carrying it away, Lambesq and I went to bring the poor ghastly head from the tower. We bore these sad remains upon our stage ; we enveloped them in the white robe that the young actor had worn some days before, when he had played the play of the Levite Zacharie in *Athalie*. We put a garland of leaves upon the head, and burned perfume about him. Moranbois went out to dig a grave for him in the village cemetery, and Bellamare returned to our actresses to inform them of what must be concealed from them no longer. It was still early ; we were surprised ; we had lived ten years since sunrise.

Léon had been a prey to keen anxiety, until the moment when he had seen the prince return. He had heard musket-shots ; but they practised firing so often in the court-yard of the manor, that he had not considered it a certain indication of our danger, and, as he had given his word not to leave the women, he had remained at his post.

He rejoined us with them on this tragic stage with Byzantine façade, which we had converted into a funeral chapel. If you wish to imagine a dramatic scene, performed as they are never acted for the public, figure to yourself the tableau that my companions of both sexes unconsciously composed. Exhausted with mental and physical fatigue, I threw myself down in a corner on the estrade, and looked at them. The women had all put on mourning. Impéria, upright, deposited a pious kiss upon the marble brow of the poor boy. The other women, kneeling, prayed around him. Bellamare, seated near the edge of the stage, was motionless and gloomy. I had seen him thus but once upon the rock. Léon was sobbing, as he leaned upon the shaft of a scenic column. Lambesq, genuinely affected, kept the perfumes burning on a beautiful tripod that the prince had lent us to figure in our tragedy; then he went from one to another, as if to speak, but he said nothing. He reproached himself for his long hostility to Marco, and seemed to feel a need of accusing himself aloud; but every one pardoned him inwardly. He had really conducted himself well in our campaign of the morning, and we no longer felt bitterness toward a man who wished to rehabilitate himself.

Moranbois returned to announce that the grave was ready. We thought that it was separating ourselves too quickly from our poor comrade, as if we were in haste to bid farewell to a mournful spectacle. We wished to pass the night in watching him. Moranbois shared our feelings, but he warned us that we had no time to lose in packing our baggage. The secret of the harem had not transpired outside; but although Nikanor had not revealed it, the guardians of the interior had guessed it, and were beginning to acquaint the dwellers in the valley with it. The murder of the two boys could not fail to be regarded as an act of justice, and their fault as execrable. More than one family professed Christianity and Islamism at the same time. In this strange country, patriotic warfare caused them to forget religious differences. It began to be known also that the prince was disappointed in his ambition, that the mountain chiefs rejected the idea of following a leader, and that his soldiers, who had flattered themselves that they would be the first in the confederation, were humiliated by his downfall. They attributed it to his French ideas, and began to have a detestation for his actors. So the prince had informed Moranbois, to whom he had just been speaking. He had advised him to bury Marco in a little cypress grove which formed part of his private domain, and not in the cemetery, where there was a waste corner for executed criminals and enemies of their religion: which?

Moranbois had not thought it best to resist. Knowing very well that, if we offended the religious customs of the country, the remains of our companion would be outraged as soon as our backs were turned, he had accepted the prince's offer, and dug the grave himself, in the place that the latter had shown him.

It was a very dense thicket, which one entered by the back door of the chapel, passing through a winding alley of laurels and cherry-trees. So we could in broad daylight and without being seen from without, transport our poor dead under this impenetrable shade. The prince had purposely withdrawn all his men from his outhouses and from that part of the domain which we should have to cross. We could deposit the body in the Greek chapel for a brief space; we even desired to do so, not that any one of us, except Régine and Anna, was a very good Christian, but we wished to render to the victim of a barbarous custom all the honors that barbarism could afford.

When we had laid the dead boy in his last bed, levelled the earth with care, and covered the spot once more with moss and withered leaves, Léon, pale and with uncovered head, began.

"Adieu, Marco," he said; "adieu to thee, the youth, the hope, the mirth, the light of our wandering family, the sweet and filial companion of our labors and of our successive miseries, of our careless joys and of our bitter disasters! This is the cruellest of our reverses, and we are about to leave thee here, alone, in an unfriendly earth, where we are forced to hide thy remains, like those of one accursed, without being permitted to leave a stone, a name, a poor flower, above the place where thou reposest.

"Poor dear child, thy father, an honest workman, unable to oppose thy ardent desire, had confided thee to us as to worthy people, and among us thou hast found fathers, uncles, brothers, and sisters; for we had all adopted thee, and we would have protected thee and guided thee in thy career and in thy life. Thou hast deserved our affection, thou hadst the most generous instincts, the most charming talents. Lost with us upon a rock amid the furious waves, thou wert, despite thy youth, one of the most devoted. An evil influence, a fatal temptation, exposed thee to a peril that thou didst defy, to a folly that thou hast expiated fearfully, but with courage and resolution, I am certain, since no cry of distress, no despairing appeal to thy comrades, broke the horrible stillness of the accursed night which has separated us forever.

"Poor dear Marco, we loved thee well, and we will cherish an ineffaceable remembrance of thee, a benediction always tender! Funereal trees, guard the secret of his last sleep beneath your shade. Be his winding-sheet, ye snows of winter and wild flowers of the spring! Birds that circle through the heavens above our heads, winged voyagers more fortunate than we, you are the sole witnesses that we can invoke! Nature, indifferent to our tears, will at least reopen her maternal bosom to that which was a body, and will carry back to God, principle of life, that which was a soul. Spirits of the earth, mysterious essences, breaths and perfumes, indefinable forces, receive the particles of generous vitality left here by this boy whom the ferocity of men has immolated; and if some unhappy exile like us should come by chance to tread upon his tomb, whisper to him softly, 'Here reposes Pierre Avenel, called Marco, murdered at eighteen years of age, far from his country, but consecrated and bedewed by the tears of his adopted family.'"

Impéria set us the example, and we all kissed the earth on the spot that hid the poor boy's forehead. We found the prince, who had waited for us in the chapel. He was sad, and I believe that he spoke sincerely to us, this time.

"My friends," said he, "I am agonized by this double murder, and, accomplished under such conditions, I regard it as a crime. You will carry away a sorry opinion of us; but take everything into consideration. I wished to introduce some civilization into this savage country. I believed that it was possible to make the idea of progress enter these heroic but hard and narrow minds. I have failed. Shall I retaliate? I do not know. Perhaps I shall bear away the palm at the moment when the Mussulman's ball shall lay me on the earth. Perhaps you will see me again in France, surfeited with perils and deceptions, consoling myself in the focus of art and letters. Whatever be the future, preserve a little regard for me. I do not regret having associated you with a generous attempt. Let Rachel be here or elsewhere, the actress who has charmed me must retain, in all security of conscience, the homage of my satisfaction and my gratitude. It is necessary that I now deprive myself of elevated pleasures, and I realize that my residence must have become odious to you. Do not wait until it is impossible, for, as you see, I am not always as absolute a master as I seem. I will give orders that to-morrow, at daybreak, your departure may be effected, without noise and without hindrance. I will give you as safe an escort as possible, but be armed at all events. I cannot accompany you; my presence would be an additional cause of irritation against you. I know that you are brave, terrible even, for you have dealt hard measure to some of my men, who thought themselves invincible. They are not to be feared at present, but they have relatives outside, and the *vendetta* is as formidable in our mountains as in those of Corsica. Be prudent, and if you hear, in your journey, some insult or some threat, do as I do often, have the appearance of not hearing it."

He next inquired where we intended to go; we had been undecided, but our resolution was taken on the instant to return to Italy. We had a horror of the East, and, in this first moment of consternation and anger, it seemed to us as if we should always have to tremble for each other there.

"If you return to Gravosa," said the prince, "my little villa is still at your disposal for whatever time you wish. Do not carry off the properties and costumes, which might embarrass and impede your progress on the mountain; I will send them after you to-morrow."

We packed our effects the same evening, and at daybreak on the morrow we presented ourselves at the drawbridge. The mules, the horses, and the men for our escort were ready on the other side of the mont; but, by a delay that seemed voluntary, they made us wait a long time for the bridge. At last we left the valley, without seeing any one, and entered the defile which penetrated far into the mountain. We were not without apprehension; if we had enemies, they would await us there. Our guides, to the number of four, rode unconcernedly before us; their horses went more swiftly than our mules, and when they were in advance they did not turn back to see if we could follow them; they continued to increase the distance between themselves and us. If we had been attacked, they probably would not have returned.

Still, we were not uneasy. We saw no hostile face, and at about three o'clock in the afternoon we had passed over two thirds of the road, and were near enough to the plain to think ourselves out of danger. We did not know that the danger lay precisely at the boundary of the prince's states.

It was much warmer than on our first passage through these mountains, and our animals threatened to refuse service. Our escort paused at last, on seeing us obliged to halt, and one of the horsemen gave us to understand, by signs, that, if we wished to drink and to water the animals, there was a stream at a little distance.

We were not thirsty; we had supplied ourselves with vials; but the beasts, and above all the one which bore our little fortune and our most valuable effects, turned obstinately in the direction of the indicated spot. We were obliged to go with them. When we saw to what a precipice they led us, we alighted, and loosened their bridles. Our guides had done the same with their horses; only one

followed them, leaping from rock to rock, to prevent them from remaining too long in the water. Moranbois held back the mule, which could not have reascended with her burden, but before he had relieved her of the cash-box, that is to say the saddle-bag that contained our funds, she escaped from his hands, and darted into the ravine.

Moranbois, fearing lest she should lose our riches, intrepidly followed her. We knew his strength and dexterity, and the place was passable, since another man ventured there. Still, we were anxious, and it was not without uneasiness that we saw him sink down and disappear under the bushes that overhung the slope. After a moment, unable to remain there, I followed him, without informing the others of my intention.

The abyss was still deeper than it had appeared; half-way down the descent became less difficult, and I began to see the bottom, when a man of repulsively dirty aspect, armed with a gun directed toward me, rushed out from behind a rock, and said to me in bad French: "You not stir, not fear, not cry, — or death. You go on, you see!"

He seized me by the arm, and led me two steps farther. Then I saw, in a perpendicular, funnel-shaped gorge, Moranbois, the fearless, invincible Moranbois, thrown down by six men who gagged and pinioned him. A score of others around them, armed with guns, pistols, and knives, rendered all hope of assistance impossible. The guide and the other animals had disappeared. Only the mule that Moranbois had followed was in the hands of these robbers, who were beginning to unload her.

I perceived it all, in the twinkling of an eye, with desperate clearness. I could not fire upon the bandits without a risk of hitting the prisoner. I quickly realized that I must remain silent.

"Not harm," continued the frightful knave who held my arm; "ransom, ransom, that is all!"

"Yes, yes," cried I, with all my might, "ransom, ransom!"

And the interpreter shouted also, probably repeating the same word to his companions in their language.

All their arms were raised directly in token of assent, and my interlocutor continued, "You leave everything up there, the beasts and the boxes, the weapons, the pocket-money, and the jewels. No harm to you!"

"But he!" I cried, pointing to Moranbois; "I demand him, or we will kill you all!"

"Have him safe and sound, make haste or him dead. Tell up there and hurry! find him at the foot of the mountain."

I went up again like a hurricane. Bellamare and Léon had heard strange voices; they came to meet me.

"Let us go back," I said to them, breathless; "help me, let us return!"

In three words all was explained, and there was not a moment's hesitation. Defence was impossible; the three guides who were left us had disappeared. Doubtless, not daring to avenge themselves, they had conducted and delivered us to the brigands of the frontier.

We left everything, even our travelling-cloaks and weapons. We threw them all upon the ground, with a feverish, delirious haste. We had but one thought, to fly with all speed to the foot of the mountain, and recover our friend. Perhaps they deceived us. They murdered him perhaps, while we were leaving all to save him. Perhaps they would assassinate us also, when they saw us alone and disarmed. No matter; one chance of safety for Moranbois and a hundred against us, we must not hesitate.

The bandit who had followed me was perched there on a rock, the loaded gun in his hands. We paid no attention to him. When he was convinced that we were carrying nothing away, and that we showed a lofty conscientiousness about it, he deigned to cry, "Thanks, Excellencies," with an air of derisive courtesy that made us depart with a nervous laugh.

"For him, for him!" cried Impéria, extending to the brigand her diamond bracelet which she was inadvertently about to carry off on her arm. "This for you! Save our friend!"

The knave leaped like a cat, took the bracelet, and wished to kiss the hand that held it out to him.

"Save him! save him!" repeated Impéria, recoiling.

"Run," replied he, "run!"

And he disappeared.

He flew like a bird, and we had a long circuit to make. At last we arrived, desperate, at the spot designated. Moranbois was there, stretched across the pathway, still gagged, unconscious, with fettered hands. We hastened to unbind him and examine him. They had kept their word to us; they had done him no injury, but the efforts that he had made to free himself had exhausted him. It was more than an hour before he regained consciousness.

We had carried him as far as the plain, for we had seen from a distance thirty brigands swooping down upon our spoils, and we feared lest they might take a fancy to deprive us of our clothes, perhaps outrage the women. Evidently they were cowards, since they had employed this *ruse*; but we were no longer formidable, thanks to the care that they had taken to make us abandon our arms.

When we found ourselves in sight of some miserable dwellings, our first thought was to hasten to them; then we feared lest they might belong to accomplices of a band who plundered travellers at so short a distance; so we rushed into a clump of box and lentisk-trees. We could carry Moranbois no longer; we could no longer support the women. We all let ourselves drop upon the ground. Moranbois recovered, and, after resting for an hour, during which time we had not exchanged a word, in the fear of drawing new enemies upon us, we resumed our journey through a dry plain strewn with stones. We wished to gain a little grove, that we perceived before us, on the right side of the road; when we arrived there it was night.

"We must stop here or die," said Bellamare. "To-morrow at daylight we shall know where we are, and we will consider. Come, my friends, let us thank God! We are his spoiled children; we have saved Moranbois!"

These words, spoken with a sublime earnestness and gayety, thrilled all the fibres of our hearts. We threw ourselves into each other's arms, crying, "Yes! yes! we are happy, and God is good!"

The Hercules burst into tears; it was probably the first time in his life.

The night was cold, and appeared long to us. We had now no cloaks to protect us, and nothing to eat or drink, after a day of terrible emotion and fatigue; but none of us thought of complaining, and none of us even consented to inform the others of his discomfort and suffering. The women were as stoical as we. The *scoglio maledetto* had case-hardened us, as Moranbois said, and we could endure a hard day and a worse night.

At daybreak we discovered where we were. The road which wound through the plain was really the way to Ragusa; we had only the Dalmatian Mountain to cross, and we took up our march again, still fasting. We encountered dwelling-houses once more; we had not a sou to pay for any breakfast whatever. We rummaged ourselves; we shook ourselves; some sleeve-buttons, overlooked in the stripping effected for the ransom, some handkerchiefs, an ear-ring,— these would pay our way until Ragusa, and we found ourselves still rich for a day. After that, it would be death or beggary, a new phase of this adventurous life which seemed to wish to spare us no evil fortune.

We saw before us a little farm,

that had somewhat the appearance of a Norman oak-grove.

"Let us knock there," said Bella-mare, "but it will not do to frighten the people, and we have a pitiful aspect. — Ladies, a little toilet, if you please ; restore some shape to your little battered hats ; fasten up with pins, if you have pins, your torn skirts. Gentlemen, retie your cravats. And you, Lawrence, draw up that bit of strap which makes you a tail. The idiots of the country are capable of taking you for a *Nyam-Nyam*."

I felt for the bit of strap and drew it up ; it was the remainder of the narrow belt which I always wore under my waistcoat, and which contained my bank-notes. Not having been able to unbuckle it quickly enough, I had grasped it impatiently, and, as it was much worn, it had broken. I had thrown upon the heap of our choicest spoils what remained in my hand, thinking to sacrifice thus conscientiously my last resource.

What was my surprise when, on looking at the portion that still hung at my side, I saw that it yet contained my five thousand francs very nearly intact!

"Miracle !" I cried ; "my friends, fortune smiles upon us, and the star of Bohemians protects us ! Here are the means for returning to France, without asking alms. Let us breakfast plentifully, if we can. I have something with which to replace the sleeve-buttons and handkerchiefs which will pay our bill, for my paper money will not pass in this desert."

We made an excellent rural repast at the house of some very hospitable people, who talked with us by signs, and who were so pleased with us that they made us go a good part of our journey in a sort of antique chariot with solid wheels that groaned infernally. Our little gifts had proved a great success.

We arrived at Ragusa in not quite as fine condition as we had left it. Our first care was to hasten to the French consulate, where I changed one of my bank-notes, and we related our sad adventure. We were told that there was no hope of recovering our fortune ; we were lucky to have preserved our lives.

It must be that the *heiduques*—that is the name they gave these brigands — were very numerous at that time, and that their bands were afraid of each other, since they had not taken time to strip us of our clothes and even of our shirts. Doubtless they had refrained from murdering us, in order not to attract the other birds of prey by the noise of a combat; they had contented themselves with our wholesale plunder, rather than share with new-comers the lesser spoils.

Lambesq, who was suspicious, thought that the prince was a party to this transaction, so as to reimburse himself; but none of us would entertain this fancy. The prince had been wrong in only one respect, apparently; this was not having furnished us with a sufficiently numerous and reliable escort : but had he not warned us that he could do no better ? And then were we certain of having been betrayed by our guides ? Seeing the brigands in force, and not wishing to lose their lives for us, three of them had fled. The fourth, the one who had been captured with Moranbois, unable to hope for a ransom for himself, must have been killed.

The chancellor of the consulate told us that our robbers were certainly strangers to the country. The natives kill for revenge, and plunder the dead only in time of war. They do not know the Italian custom of ransom. I remembered that the knave with whom I had been forced to compromise had a face and accent entirely different from the people of the country.

All conjectures were, however, very useless; we were ruined, irretrievably. We arranged for our departure the next day. We did not wish to make capital of our mishap by beating the big drum, that we might make money in the country; we were, besides, too much fatigued to set at work again. The next day we received our costumes and properties that the prince had sent us, without suspecting our misfortunes. Doubtless, had he known them, he would have offered us some recompense; and perhaps we might have accepted it, if it had not been for the memory of our poor Marco, which now stood between us and his munificence. We could not even write to him what had happened to us. If he treated our guides with severity, a rebellion might break out against him. There were victims enough already. We had only one desire, to leave, as soon as possible, this country, which had proved so disastrous to us.

We bought some clothes and engaged our passage on the Austrian *Lloyd* steamer for Trieste. While dining at the only hotel of the town, and talking of our last adventure, Moranbois told us that it cost us dearer than it was worth.

"Hush," said Bellamare, "nothing is worth so much as a brave man, and nothing is better for the health than a brisk movement! See, my well-beloved strollers, are we not happier since that time than we were on leaving that fortress of misfortune? We took away a fortune that truly was too bitter for us! We had occasion to detest the savages who had given it to us, at the cost of one of our dearest heads. Every enjoyment that this money might have procured us would have oppressed our hearts like a remorse, and we could never have amused ourselves without seeing the pale face of Marco in the midst of us. Now, this face will smile upon us, for, if the brave boy could return, he would say to us, 'Weep no more; what you could not do to save me, you have done for another, and, this time, you have succeeded.' Come, Moranbois, be no longer sad. Is it because, for the first time in your life, you have been *thrown*, my Hercules? Had you expected to knock down thirty men, single-handed? Is it as cashier that you sigh? What is there so out of order in our finances? When we left here, five weeks since, we had no great amount; we felt very proud of earning so much in so short a time it was not natural, it could not last; but here we are, still upon our feet, since we have our implements of labor, our properties, and our costumes. One of us finds his old floating capital again, by a miracle. We are going to rest ourselves at sea, to salute the *scoglio maledetto* in passing, and laugh in its face; after which we will perform, and we shall all have talents of the first order; you will see! Purpurin himself shall recite verses correctly. What would you have! We have suffered much together, and the hours of devotion have ennobled us. We have earned something more than wealth, we have become better. We love each other more; we shall still quarrel at rehearsals, perhaps, but we feel sure in advance that we shall pardon each other everything, and that we can disagree without ceasing to love each other. Come! Since the departure from Saint Clement, all is for the best, and I drink to the health of the brigands!"

The word of Bellamare had a sovereign influence over our minds, and I know of no discouragement from which it would not have lifted us. We were, like all actors, very mocking and facetious with each other; but he, the most mocking and facetious of all, had so ardent a conviction on serious occasions, that he rendered us enthusiastic as himself.

So we had not a regret for our vanished fortune, and Moranbois had to follow the example of the others.

During our passage we all had the expectation of seeing the *scoglio maledetto* again. We should certainly have recognized it among a thousand; but we did not pass it, or we passed it in the night. In vain we questioned the crew and the passengers: they could not inform us, since we had christened the island at random,

and none of us were sufficiently versed in geography to set competent people on the track. Two or three times, we fancied that it appeared to us in the evening mist: it was a dream. Where we thought we saw familiar outlines there was nothing.

"Let us preserve this rock in our imagination," said Léon. "There it will be still more terrible and beautiful than the real vision would represent it to us."

"More beautiful?" cried Régine; "you found it beautiful, did you? Poets are mad enough!"

"No," replied Léon, "poets are wise; they are, in fact, the only wise ones who exist. When others are disturbed and frightened, they dream and contemplate; even while suffering, they see; they have the enjoyment of regarding and appreciating until their last hour. Yes, my friends, it was a splendid place, and I have never understood the fascination of the sea so perfectly as during that week of anguish, when we were face to face and side by side with it, always threatened and insulted by its blind wrath, always protected by that rock which it has assailed for incalculable ages, without being able to devour it. We were, nevertheless, in the very bowels of the monster; and I often thought, at that time, of the legend of Jonah in the whale. Doubtless the Prophet was cast like us upon a rock. In his day they related everything in metaphor, and perhaps his refuge had the fantastic form of the Scriptural leviathan; perhaps, like us, he might have hollowed out a grotto to shelter himself, during his three days and three nights of ship-wreck."

"Your explanation is ingenious," said Bellamare; "but relate to us, then, your impressions of seven days and seven nights in the bowels of the rock, for, as for me, I confess to not having had the wisdom to admire anything except our persistency in not wishing to die there."

"To relate contemplations, interrupted every moment by the suffering of others, is impossible," responded Léon. "You did not wish to die, and each of you was providentially sustained by some instinct or by some ruling thought. Régine desired to gain her safety in order to fast no longer; Lucinde felt that she was still too handsome to throw up the game; Anna —"

"Ah! as for me," said Anna, "I was sustained by nothing. I was resigned to dying."

"No! since you cried with fear at the approach of death."

"I cried without knowing why; however, when I calmed myself, it was with the thought of seeing once more, in another world, the two poor little children that I have lost. But let us speak of the others, if it makes no difference to you!"

"For my part," said Bellamare, "I thought of you all, and never have I appreciated you all so well. My friendship for you mingled with my artistic sentiment, and I kept repeating, often involuntarily, this reflection, which would not leave my head, 'What a pity that there is not an enlightened public there, to see how fine and dramatic they are!' Seriously, I mechanically noted all the effects. I studied the rags, the posés, the groups, the aberrations, the accent, the color, and the form of all these scenes of despair, heroism, and madness."

"And I," said Impéria, "I heard, continually, a mysterious music in the wind and in the waves. In proportion as I became weaker, this music assumed more connection and intensity. A time came, it was during the last days, when I could notice admirable measures and sublime harmonies."

"As for me," said Lambesq, "I was irritated at the dry noise made by the stones heaped up by our labors in the beginning; when the wind scattered them, it was like the derisive plaudits of a dissatisfied audience, and I was furious with the head of the 'claque,' who let our success go adrift."

"You see plainly," replied Léon, "that you were all bound to life by the force of habit or the obstinacy of your specialty. So it is not astonishing that, until the moment when I saw the tartan sailing toward us, and the form of Moranbois standing upon the deck, I should have been preoccupied and sustained by the wish to admire and to describe. That archipelago where we were imprisoned; those bare and jagged rocks, which at their base took all the green reflections of the sea, and at their summit all the ethereal hues of heaven; those irregular, forbidding, cruel forms of desert islands that we could not reach, and that seemed to summon us like instruments of torture, that they might grind and tear us under their sharp teeth; — all this was so grand and so threatening, that I felt eager to measure myself by poetry with these terrible things. The more I realized our abandonment and powerlessness, the more I thirsted to crush by the genius of inspiration those gloomy giants of stone and that insatiable fury of the waves. I was indifferent to death, since I had had time to compose a masterpiece and inscribe it on the rock."

"And this masterpiece?" cried I. "You composed it? you will repeat it to us!"

"Alas!" responded Léon, "I believed I did so! Not having strength to cut the rock with a knife, I wrote it in my album. I guarded it sacredly in my breast, during the days of stupefaction which succeeded our deliverance. I endeavored to read it again in secret; I did not understand it; and I persuaded myself that it was in consequence of the state of physical weakness to which I was reduced. When I felt restored and strengthened, at the house of Prince Klémenti, I discovered, with horror, that my verses were not verses. There was neither rhyme nor metre; the idea, even, had no sense. It was the product of a complete mental alienation. I consoled myself by the reflection that this madness of rhyming even in agony had, at least, rendered me insensible to suffering and superior to despair."

"My children," said Bellamare, "if we do not discover our rock in this passage it is probable that we shall never have either the time or the opportunity to find it. Does it not seem incredible to you that within two days' distance of Italy, in the midst of civilized Europe, upon a narrow sea, continually frequented, explored in every portion, we have been lost upon an unknown island, as if we had been in quest of some new land, on a voyage of exploration toward the Poles? This adventure is so improbable that we shall never dare relate it. They will not believe us when we say that the captain and the two sailors died, unable to tell the name of the rock, not knowing it, probably, and that those who brought us away from it, and who must have informed us, did not find one of us capable of understanding and remembering it. I confess that, for my own part, I was completely idiotic. I still acted mechanically. I cared for you all, and Impéria assisted me. Léon and our poor Marco also busied themselves with the sick; but it would be impossible for me to say how many times we took to reach Ragusa, and I certainly passed two days there before knowing in what country we were, and without thinking to inquire."

"I will confess the same thing," said Impéria; "and Léon was still longer so, I wager."

"Do you know," replied Léon, "that we have, perhaps, dreamed this shipwreck? Who can swear that what he sees and hears is real?"

"I have heard," said Bellamare, "of a metaphysical or religious belief of the ancient East, which held that nothing exists but God. Our passage on the earth, our emotions, our passions, our griefs, and our joys, all this was only vision, effervescence of some intellectual chaos; latent world which aspired to be, but which fell back incessantly into nothingness, to lose itself in the sole reality, which is God."

"I understand nothing of all that," said Régine, "but I assure you that I did not dream the hunger and thirst on the accursed rock. Every time that I think of it, I have almost a bell ringing in my stomach."

We arrived at Trieste, without having perceived the rock. On inspecting geographical charts, we thought, and were told that we must have been stranded on the *scoglio pomo*, in the middle of the sea, or the Lagostini, nearer to Ragusa; but we must remain in perpetual uncertainty, more especially as some learned man gave us another explanation that better pleased our excited imaginations. According to him, our shipwreck coinciding with the shock of earthquake which was felt upon the coasts of Illyria, the undiscoverable rock must, at that moment, have issued spontaneously from the sea, and then have sunk back into it. Thus, we had not only been threatened with dying of hunger and cold, but we might, besides, at any moment, disappear below, like the condemned demons of an operatic *dénouement*.

On leaving Trieste, where we played *Les Folies Amoureuses, Quitte pour la Peur, Les Caprices de Marianne. Bataille de Dames,* we strolled about the North of Italy, enlisting as coadjutors a French troupe, some members of which were passable. Those who were good for nothing swelled our number, and we could extend our repertory and undertake pieces containing many characters,— *Trente Ans ou la Vie d'un Joueur, Le*

Comte Hermann, etc. We were tolerably successful, and the public appeared very well satisfied with us. Nevertheless, the profession lost much of its charm for me. The new company was so different from ours! The women had impossible morals, the men intolerable manners. They were genuine strollers, eaten up with vanity, irritable, coarse, quarrelsome, indelicate, drunken. Each of them had one or two of these vices; some possessed them all at once. They understood nothing of our mode of life, and laughed at us for it. I had been reared among peasants rude enough; but they were people of good breeding in comparison with these. And all that did not prevent them from knowing how to wear a costume, moving on the stage with a certain elegance, and concealing the hiccups of drunkenness under a grave or excited air.

In the greenroom they were odious to us. Régine, alone, kept them respectful by her cool and unrestrained derison. Lambesq, at rehearsal, threw the properties at their heads. Moranbois restored them to their places by main force. Bellamare pitied them for having fallen so low from excessive poverty and weariness of their deceptions. He strove to raise them again in their own eyes, to make them realize that the misery of their condition arose from their idleness, their want of conscientiousness in performance and of respect toward the audience. They heard him with astonishment, sometimes with a little emotion; but they were incorrigible.

It became evident to me that mediocrity on the stage inevitably leads to ruin those who have not an exceptional moral worth, and I asked myself if, deprived of the direction of Bellamare and the influence of Impéria and Léon, who were, themselves, exceptional characters, I should not have sunk as low as these unfortunate actors. The personal qualities of the managers of these wandering troupes were worst of all. The almost continual lack of success reduced them to perpetual bankruptcy. They made up their mind to it, with a shameful philosophy, and did not shrink from any breach of faith to regain their footing. They inquired by what miracle Bellamare had preserved his spotless name and his honorable connection. It never entered their minds to consider that he had had no other secret than that of being an honest man to gain on all occasions the support of honest people.

It was long before we separated from this heterogeneous element; and when we were once more in France, alone by ourselves, we experienced a great relief. We replaced Marco by a pupil from the Conservatory, who could not secure an engagement in Paris, and who had no talent of his own, since he confined himself to aping Régnier. Régine and Lucinde remained with us as *pensionnaires*, and Lambesq asked to be a member of the association. We did not hesitate to admit him. He had, certainly, incorrigible defects, an immense vanity, a puerile captiousness, and a self-love which was extraordinary from its openness; but he had, however, gained wisdom from

adversity, and, after having excited our indignation at the time of the shipwreck, he had atoned for his misconduct at Saint Clément and on the mountain. He had reflected on the inconvenience of selfishness. His heart was not entirely cold; he was attached to us. He went so far as to make proposals of marriage to Anna, who had, at one time, wished to be his wife, but whom he had deceived. Since then, however, she had loved several others, and she refused, while thanking him, and promising him a faithful friendship.

In connection with this subject, Anna, who had a habit of never alluding to the past, explained her feelings to me in a chance *tête-à-tête*. I desired to know what she thought of Léon, and if the stifled regrets of the latter had any substantial foundation.

"I do not like," she told me, "to look back. There are only sorrows and disappointments for me there. I am very impressible, and I should have died ten times, if I had not a supreme resource in my character, which is to forget; I have often believed myself in love, but, in reality, I have loved only my first lover, this madman of a Léon, who might have made a faithful wife of me, if he had not been excessively jealous and suspicious. He was very unjust to me; he believed that Lambesq was his rival at a time when he was nothing of the sort; then I attached myself to Lambesq, through pique, and after that to others through *ennui*, caprice, or despair. Think of that, Lawrence; one sports with love, when one can call it fancy; but there are fancies of intrigue that are gay, and there are those that are tragic, because they arise from fear of remembrance and horror of loneliness. Never laugh at me, then ; you do not know the pain you give me, you who are better than the others, and who, not loving me, would not feign to love me, to make me commit another indiscretion ! If Léon sometimes speaks of me to you, tell him that my absurd and broken life is his work and that his distrust has ruined me. Now, it is too late. I have only to forgive, with a gentleness that they take for unconcern, and which will doubtless finish by becoming that."

Our life began again to be what it had always been before our disasters, —a lively journey without loss or profits, a pellmell of feverish occupation and wasted time, a whole of kind relations interspersed with little quarrels and warm reconciliations. This life, without repose and without reflection, gradually converts the provincial actor into a being who may be considered, not as in a chronic state of drunkenness, but always half inebriated. The theatre and travelling stimulate like spirits. The soberest among us were often the most irritable.

In the beginning of the winter, I received a letter which broke off my artistic career, and decided my life. My godmother, a good woman who sells groceries here, wrote to me: "Come quickly. Your father is dying !"

We were then at Strasburg. I scarcely took time to embrace my comrades, and departed. I found my father out of danger. But he had had a stroke of apoplexy, in consequence of violent emotion, and my godmother related what had happened to me.

No one, in my little town, had ever suspected the profession that I had embraced. The people here do not travel for pleasure. They have no affairs abroad, being all descended from five or six families, rooted in the soil for ages. If the younger ones sometimes wish to go to Paris, that is all. I had never played at Paris, and the troupe — we called ourselves the "Bellamare Society"— had never had occasion to approach my province. So I had not even taken the trouble to conceal my name, which was not peculiar enough to attract attention, and which served very well in my line of characters.

It happened, however, that a commercial traveller, with whom I had become acquainted in his passage through Auvergne, during my vacation of the preceding year, arrived at Turin at the same time with us, and recognized my face on the stage and my name on the poster. He tried to see me at the *café* where I sometimes went after the performance ; but I did not go there that evening. He departed the next day, and I lost the opportunity to request him to keep it secret, in case he should revisit Arvers.

He passed through there two months later, and did not fail to inquire about me. No one could tell him where I was or what I was doing. Then, either from a love of talking or a desire to reassure my anxious friends, he informed them of the truth. He had seen me, with his own eyes, upon the boards.

At first the news caused only a stupefied surprise, and then came comments and questions. They wished to know if I earned much money, and if I was making a fortune. To make a fortune is, in Auvergne, the criterion of good and evil. A profession that enriches is always honorable; a profession that does not enrich is always disgraceful. The commercial traveller did not scruple to tell them that I was on the road to starvation, and that, since I liked to travel, I should have done better to go about selling wines.

The news made the circuit of the little town directly, and even reached my father, before the end of the day. You remember that he applied the term *comedian* * to leaders of bears and swallowers of swords. He shrugged his shoulders, and denounced as liars those who thus calumniated me. He sought out the commercial traveller, at this very inn, and tried to understand the matter. Delighted to assume a little importance in the eyes of an alarmed father and an astonished population, our good man rehabilitated me somewhat by saying that I did not juggle with little balls, and that I did not dance the tight-rope; but he declared that my existence was very precarious, that probably I was in a way to acquire all the vices that an adventurous life engenders, and that it

* The French word *comedian* is a general term applied to actors, and does not necessarily imply one who performs a comic part. —*Translator's Note.*

would be rendering me a service to remove me from a profession which was leading me astray or making money out of me.

My poor father withdrew, very sad and very thoughtful; but he had such confidence in me, that he did not wish to tell me his first impression. With the patience of the peasant who knows how to wait until the corn sprouts and ripens, he would leave it until my next letter. I wrote him every month, and my letters always tended to preserve his security. I had not related my terrible adventures to him, and I had only to render him a good account of my studies, without telling him their nature and object.

He regained confidence. I was a good son; I could not deceive him. If I was a *comedian*, it was doubtless something honorable and wise, of which he could not judge; but a little sadness still lingered in his heart, and he was more constant in his attendance at church in order to pray for me.

With great religious faith, he had never been devout. He became so, and the *curé* gained an ascendency over him. Then, by degrees, his anxiety was aroused and sustained. They combated his trustful apathy; they represented me to him as a lost sheep, then as a hardened sinner; at last, one day, they told him that, if he did not snatch me from the claws of Satan, I should be damned; that I should have a shameful, perhaps a terrible death; and that I should not be buried in holy ground, but thrown to the vultures.

This was the last blow for him.

He returned home heart-broken, and next day he was found almost dead in his bed. The sacristan, who was his particular friend, my poor godmother, who is a good-natured fool, and Mother Ouchafol, who is an ill-natured fool, had contributed not a little by their silly talk and their absurd ideas to dishearten and kill my father.

When I saw him out of danger, I swore to him that I would never leave him without his full and entire permission, and he resumed his spade. I imposed silence on our stupid friends, and I endeavored to make my father understand and accept the resolution that I had taken to be an actor. It was not easy; he had been struck with deafness in his illness, and his mind had not yet become clear. I saw that reflection wearied him, and that a secret anxiety retarded his complete recovery. I began to work in the garden, and pretended to take great pleasure in it; his face brightened, and I saw that a thorough revolution had taken place in his ideas. Formerly, desirous that I should be a gentleman, he had not allowed me even to touch his farming implements. Now, thinking me damned if I returned to the stage, he saw safety and honor for me only in manual labor and in soldering my life to the soil where he had riveted his own.

All my attempts were fruitless. He did not find a word to argue with me, but he hung his head, grew pale, and went dejectedly to his bed. I gave it up. That unalterable gentleness, that heart-rending silence, only proved to me, too strongly, the impossibility of his understanding me, and the invincible power of the fixed idea, damnation. When a generous and tender soul like his has been able to admit this odious belief, it is forever closed.

The physicians had warned me of the probability of one or more relapses, probably serious. I would not risk hastening their return and I submitted; I became gardener.

Nevertheless, I wished to bid adieu to my other family, to Bellamare and Impéria especially. I learned by chance that they were at Clermont; and, as I had left a portion of my effects in their keeping, I easily obtained some days of freedom from my father to settle up my affairs outside, assuring him that I would return at the end of the week.

I found the company beneath their accustomed shelter; they had been unwilling to touch the last bank-notes that I had left in the cash-box. I insisted that they should use them, and that they should repay me only by small instalments, when they could without giving themselves any anxiety in regard to it. I pretended that I had no need of the money; that, condemned to stay indefinitely in my village, I had more than sufficient resources of my own. I told a falsehood; there remained to me absolutely nothing. I would not confess it to my father; I would only ask to share his roof and his bread, as the price of my daily labor.

But before leaving Impéria, I wished to have done with the tenacious hope that I had never been able to overcome, and I requested her to hear me, without distraction or interruption, in the presence of Bella-mare. She consented, not without an uneasiness that she could not conceal from me. Bellamare said to her, before me: "My child, I know very well what is to be the subject; I divined it a long time ago. You must listen to Lawrence without alarm or prudery, and reply to him without reticence or mystery. I do not know your secrets; I have no motive and no right to question you; but Lawrence ought to know them, appreciate them, and govern his future conduct by them. Let us all three go away into the country; I will leave you to talk alone. I do not wish to have any opinion, any influence whatever, before Lawrence has spoken to you freely, and with open heart."

We entered a little shady nook, where flowed a limpid stream, and Bellamare left us, telling us that he would return in two hours.

Impéria produced upon me the effect of a victim resigned to the grievous trial of a long-dreaded and perfectly useless confidence.

"I see plainly," I said to her, "that you have guessed also, that you pity me, and that you will never love me; but a drowning man catches at whatever he can grasp, until the last moment, and I am going to enter on an existence which is intellectual death, if I do not carry into it a little hope. Do not then think it useless that I desire to prepare myself for a shipwreck, perhaps worse than that of the Adriatic."

Impéria covered her face with her hands and burst into tears.

"I know," I said, kissing her wet hands, "that you have a friendship, a true friendship for me."

"Yes," said she, "a deep, immeasurable friendship. Yes, Lawrence, when you tell me that I do not love you, you do me a frightful wrong. I am not cold, I am not selfish, I am not ungrateful, I am not foolish. Your affection for me has been generous indeed; you have never let me see it, except in spite of yourself, in rare moments of fever and of excitement. When you expressed it to me passionately on the rock, you were mad, you were dying. Afterwards, and almost always, you repressed and conquered it so well that I thought you absolutely cured. I know that you have done everything to forget me, and to make me believe that you cared for me no longer. I know that you plunged recklessly into distractions that were, perhaps, not really worthy of you, and from which you emerged gloomy and almost desperate. More than once, without your knowledge, your eyes have said to me, 'If I am dissatisfied with myself, it is your fault. It was only necessary to give me hope; and I should have been constant and faithful.' Yes, my dear Lawrence, yes, I know all that, and all that you would say to me I could suggest to you. Perhaps, if you had been faithful to me without hope — But no, no, I will not tell you that; that would be too romantic, and perhaps untrue; you would have been still more perfect than you are; you would have been a hero of chivalry. I should even have fallen in love with you; it would have been necessary to conquer it or yield to it; to conquer it, which is a great grief for you; to yield to it, which would have been a remorse and a despair for me. Listen, Lawrence; I am not free, I am married."

"Married!" I cried, "you married! It is not true!"

"It is not literally true; but in my own eyes I am irrevocably bound. I have pledged my conscience and my life to an oath which is my strength and my religion. I really love some one, and I have loved him for five years."

"It is not true," I repeated angrily; "that fable is worn out; that pretext can serve no longer. You told Bellamare, before me, at Paris, one day when I was still sick, and when I pretended to be asleep, that it was not true."

"You heard that!" replied she, blushing. "Ah well, it is an additional reason."

"Explain yourself."

"Impossible. All that I can tell you is that I conceal my secret, especially from Bellamare. It is to him that I lie and that I shall lie, all the necessary time. It is he who might guess, and I do not wish him to guess."

"Then it is Léon that you love?"

"No, I assure you that it is not Léon. I have never thought of him; and as after him there is only Lambesq to suppose, I beg you to spare me the humiliation of denying, and to put no more useless questions to me. I have been sincere with you, always! Do not punish me by your distrust! Do not make me suffer more than I suffer already."

"Ah well, my friend, be sincere even to the end; tell me if you are happy, if you are loved?"

She refused to answer me, and I lost command of my will; this incomprehensible mystery exasperated me. I complained of it with so much energy, that I drew from her a portion of the truth, in consonance, alas! with what Impéria had told me, with a half-serious tone, at Orleans, on the road which led to the Vachard villa. She had never revealed her love to the one who was the object of it; he did not even suspect it. She was sure that he would be happy, when she should make it known to him; but this day had not yet come; she had two or three years yet to wait for it. She wished to preserve herself free and irreproachable, in order to give confidence to this man who shrank from marriage. Where was this man? what was he doing? where and when did she see him? Impossible to make her say. When I hazarded the supposition that he was not far from the place inhabited by Impéria's father, and that she met him there, every year, when she went to see this infirm father, she replied, "Perhaps," but with a tone that seemed to me to signify, "Believe that if you like, you will never guess."

I gave it up, but then, I did all that is humanly possible to show her how insane was this romantic passion. She was sure of nothing in the future, not even of pleasing, and she sacrificed her youth to a dream, to a resolution which resembled a monomania.

"Ah well," replied she, "that is like the love you have for me. From the beginning you have known that I loved some one who was absent. I said so very distinctly, the first time that you looked at me with too expressive eyes in the greenroom of the Odéon. I have repeated it to you at every opportunity, and it is true. Unable to have my love, you wished for my friendship. You obtained it. You have it. You have contented yourself with it for three years; you would not have exchanged it for the agitations that would have troubled us uselessly. You know that I should have fled. You were happy with us, even through the greatest miseries and the most mournful trials. We all loved each other dearly; and, confess it, there were days, weeks, whole months perhaps, when we were so excited, so exalted, that you congratulated yourself on being only my friend You would not have wished, at those times, to see me exchange our chivalric brotherhood for the ardors and the fancies in which poor Anna consumes herself. Ah well, my life is idolatrous as yours; an idea, a secret preference, a dream of the future, have made us both insane, and we should understand and pardon each other. You say that I am your fixed idea; permit me, also, to have my serious, incurable madness. We have no really social existence; we are outside all conventions, good or bad, that reason suggests to prudent and steady people. Their logic is not ours. Prejudice disappears in vain; we form a band apart, and those who know us well will say of us that we are, with mystic devotees, the last disciples of an extra-social, extra-practical, extra-human ideal.

To any man, bound to the world as it exists, one can say, 'Where are you going? to what does that lead you?' This man, if he is ready to commit great follies, stops, desperate, and sees before him only shame or suicide. As for us, when they ask us where we are going, we answer, laughing, that we go on that we may not stand still, and our future is always full of phantoms that laugh more loudly than we. Discouragement seizes us only when we can no longer count on chance. Do not tell me, then, that I am mad. I know it well since I became an actress, and you are mad, also, since you became an actor. You needed an idol; I had needed one, before I knew you; we have met too late."

It seemed to me that she was right, and I argued no longer; I was even embarrassed when she asked where we should be, if I had succeeded in making her love me.

"Are you free? Do you not belong to a duty, a country, a father, a labor different from ours? Have you not committed a great folly in attaching yourself to us, who have no longer either country or family or duty outside our wandering fold? Have you not prepared a boundless chagrin for yourself, in giving us some years of your youth, knowing that you would be forced to separate from us? What would you do with me, at this moment if I were your wife? I do not know whether you have really a competency, and that would make no difference to me, since we could work together; but could we? Could you even give me an asylum from which they would not chase me as a vagabond? Would not the meanest of your peasants think he had a right to scorn and to insult Mademoiselle de Valclos, the *baladine?* You see plainly that you ought to think yourself fortunate in not having assumed duties toward me that you could not fulfil."

"But," I answered, "I did not come to ask your hand; it seemed to me that your heart was free, and you could say to me, 'Hope and return!' My poor father has, they tell me, but a few years, perhaps few months, to live. I intend to devote myself to prolonging his existence as far as possible, and that without regret, without hesitation, without impatience. I do not feel dismayed at my task; I shall perform it, whatever be the future; but the future, it is you, Impéria, and you are not willing that my devotion aspires to a reward? I have often told you that I should inherit a fortune, small indeed, but quite sufficient to continue, and perhaps consolidate, our association. I should have joyfully accepted this community of interests with Bellamare and his friends—"

"No," said Impéria, "Bellamare would not have accepted it. All that is useless, my good Lawrence. Let us not mingle the interests of the world with those of Bohemia. Bellamare will never borrow except to repay, and it is himself alone who can save Bellamare."

"It would at least be permitted me," I replied, "to remain united to his destiny and yours. You will not, then, even leave me the hope of repeating our campaigns, and once more becoming your brother?"

"Within a short time, no," she said; "you would suffer too much from the explanation that we have just been having; but some day, when you have entirely forgiven me for not loving you, when you yourself shall love another woman,— but another woman will not wish that you should leave her, and you see— We turn round in a circle, since for your future happiness it is necessary that you break with the present, and that you renounce it without reservation. I should be very culpable, if I told you the contrary."

Each of her words fell on my heart like clods of earth on a coffin. I was annihilated, and suddenly there arose a violent reaction in me. I felt like the prisoner who breaks his chains, if only to take some steps before he dies. I expressed my love to her with the violence of despair, and again she wept bitterly, telling me that I was pitiless, that I tortured her. Her grief, which was real and which choked her, deceived me for a moment. I persuaded myself that she loved me, and that she was sacrificing herself to a cruel duty. Yes, I swear to you that she seemed to love me, to regret me, and to fear my caresses, for she withdrew her hands from me; and if sometimes, overcome, she concealed her face upon my shoulder, she started back as suddenly, like a woman on the point of yielding. She was neither deceitful nor cold nor coquettish: I knew it, I was sure of it, after so long an intimacy and so many opportunities of seeing her generous character in every sort of trial. I grew mad.

"Sacrifice your oath to me," I said; "forget the man to whom you owe it. For my part, I will sacrifice all to you; I will leave my father to die alone and hopeless. Love is above all human laws; it is all; it can create all and destroy all. Be mine, and let the universe crumble around us!"

She repulsed me gently, but with a mournful air.

"You see," said she, "where passion leads those who listen to it; they blaspheme and they lie! You would abandon your father no more than I would abandon my friend. We should forget them for a day, perhaps; on the morrow we should leave each other, to rejoin them, and if we did not we should despise each other. Leave me, Lawrence; if I listened to you, our love would kill our friendship and our mutual esteem. I swear to you, for my part, that, the day I lose my self-respect, I will do justice to myself, I will kill myself!"

She went to rejoin Bellamare, who reappeared at the entrance of the ravine, and I suffered her to leave me without detaining her. All was over for me, and I entered on a phase of the most utter indifference to life.

Bellamare led Impéria away, after having requested me to wait for him; he had something to say to me. When he returned, he found me riveted to the same spot, in the same attitude, my eyes fixed on the stream, whose little eddies against the stone I was following mechanically, without remembering myself.

"My child," he said to me, as he sat down beside me, "will you, can you relate to me what has passed between her and yourself? Do you think that you may tell me? I have no right to question you, I repeat; having never been in love with her, I am not authorized to ask of her a positive reply like that which you have just required. She tells me, now as always, that she does not wish to love, and — I owe you the truth, she shows so much grief, that it seems to me that she loves you in spite of herself. It must be that there is an obstacle that it is impossible for me to conjecture. If it is a secret which she has confided to you, do not tell me; but if it is a simple confidence, take me for adviser and for judge. Who knows if I cannot overcome the obstacle, and restore you to hope?"

I related to him all that she had said to me. He reflected, questioned again, sought conscientiously, and found nothing which could explain the mystery. He was even vexed by it. Intelligent, experienced, penetrating as he was, he saw before him, he said, a veiled statue with an indecipherable inscription.

"Let us see," he resumed, in conclusion, "one must never say that a thing is ended. Nothing ends in life. It is never necessary to forswear an affection nor to bury one's own heart. I do not wish you to go away broken or ruined. A man is not a wall, whose stones are crushed upon the road; or a pipe, whose fragments are thrown away at a street corner. The fragments of an intellect are always good. You will return home, and take care of your father; you will do everything he wishes, — water his flower-beds and prune his fruit trees, — and you will think of the future as of a thing which belongs to you, which is due to you, and of which you will dispose. You know well that on the *scoglio maledetto* I made plans until the last hour, and that they are realized. Go, then, my child, and do not imagine that I accept your resignation as artist. I shall work for you, I shall question Impéria. Now, I must and will know her secret. When I know it, I shall write to you, 'Stay away forever!' or, 'Return as soon as you can!' If she loves you, ah well, it is not so impossible for you to see each other occasionally, unknown to your people. There are always means, if your exile must be prolonged, of rendering it supportable, were it only by mutual confidence and the certainty of meeting again. Go away, then, with an easy mind; nothing is changed in your situation; this doubt that you have endured for three years you can still endure for three weeks, for I engage that you shall know your fate at the end of that time."

This admirable friend succeeded in restoring me to a little courage, and I departed without seeing either Impéria or the others, in order not to lose what little energy was left me. When I was once more at home, I wrote to him to beg him to spare me if he should learn the certainty of my unhappiness. " In that case," I said to him, " write me nothing. I will wait; I will lose my last hope gradually, and without violence."

I waited three weeks; I waited three months; I waited three years. He did not write to me. I have ceased to hope.

I have had one consolation: my father has recovered his health; he is no longer threatened with apoplexy; he is calm; he thinks me happy, and he is happy.

I have forsworn all my artistic dreams, and, wishing to have done with regrets, I have unreservedly become a laborer. I have striven to be again the peasant that I ought to be. I have never reproached my father for having twice sacrificed me, — the first time to his ambition, the second to his devotion. He has not understood his error; he is innocent of it; I revenge myself for it by loving him the more. I have a need of loving; my nature is like that of a faithful dog. My father is the child who is intrusted to me and whom I guard: or, rather, I have the nature of a lover; I need to serve and protect some one; the old man is devoted to me; it is my duty to watch over him and to spare him every grief, every danger, every anxiety. I am grateful to him for being unable to do without me; I thank him for having fettered me.

You may well believe that I have not acquired this resignation in a day; I have suffered much! The life that I lead here is the antipodes of my tastes and aspirations; but I prefer it to the paltry bourgeois ambitions that they would suggest to me. I would not take the slightest situation; I will have no other chain than that of love and my own will. The one I bear wounds me sometimes to my very blood; but it is for my father that I bleed, and I will not bleed for a sub-prefect, a mayor, or even a comptroller of finance. If I were tax-collector, my dear monsieur, I should regard you as a superior, and I should not open my heart to you, as I am doing at this moment. Bellamare told me truly; when one has devoted himself to the theatre, he never recovers from it. He cannot find his place in the world again'; he has represented too many fine personages to accept the low employments of modern civilization. I have been Achilles, Hypolite, and Tancred, by costume and by figure; I have stammered the language of the demigods; I should not know how to be either clerk or registrar. I should think myself travestied, and should be still worse as an employee than I was as an actor. In the time of Molière, they had a theatrical situation specified thus, "Such a one plays the kings and the peasants." I have often thought of this contrast which sums up my life and continues as my fiction, for I am no more peasant than I am monarch. I am forever unclassed, imitating the life of others, and having no existence of my own.

Happy love would have made me man as well as an artist. A beautiful lady dreamed of transforming me entirely; it was undertaking too much; she would, perhaps, have created the man; she would have killed the artist. Impéria would do neither; it was her right. I love her still; I shall love her always; but I have sworn to leave her in peace. I submit to it, not passively, that is possible only in appearance, but with a secret exaltation that I reveal to no one. Perhaps I display therein the vanity of the strolling player who loves lofty rôles, but I act my play without the support of any public. When this exaltation grows too strong, I become the actor, that is to say, the rhapsodist, the merry-maker, the singer of village ballads with my village comrades. I drink, occasionally, to shake off my trouble; and when my imagination wings its flight too high, I make love to ugly girls, who are not cruel, and do not force me to lie in order to please them.

This will last as long as the life of my father, and I ought to adopt a well-tempered philosophy to preserve me from the sacrilegious desire of his death. I never allow myself, then, to think of what I shall become when I have lost him. Upon my honor, monsieur, I know nothing of it, and I do not wish to know.

So there you have the explanation how the man whom you saw half intoxicated yesterday at the tavern is the same who relates to you to-day a most romantic history. It is true in all respects, and I have told you only the principal events, in order not to tire your patience.

Here Lawrence finished his recital and left me, deferring till to-morrow the pleasure of hearing my reflections. It was two o'clock in the morning.

My reflections were neither long nor formal. I admired this devoted nature. I loved this generous and upright heart. I did not quite understand his persistency in loving a woman either cold or with preoccupied affections. I was established in the very midst of the existing social state. I had no romantic instincts;

it was, perhaps, on that account that the story of Lawrence had strongly interested me; for interest always springs, to a considerable extent, from astonishment, and a narrator who regarded things from the self-same stand-point as his auditor would not entertain him in the least, I am certain.

The only observation that I could make to Lawrence was as follows: "You will not end your life in the condition to which you now submit. You will no sooner be free, than you will return to the stage, or seek to enter the world. Do not deaden your capability for enjoyment; do not undermine your admirable constitution by excess."

But he feared so much to hear of the future, the word alone damped him so suddenly, that I dared not even pronounce it. I saw plainly that his sacrifice caused him still more sadness than he was willing to avow; and that the idea of a liberty which he would obtain only on the death of his father inspired him with profound terror and anxiety.

I only permitted myself to tell him that, if he must be gardener all his life, it was no more necessary to debase himself in that condition than in any other; and I was so much the more eloquent, that I had been overtaken on the preceding evening by undeniable intoxication. He promised to regulate himself and overcome those moments of weakness when he estimated himself too cheaply. He thanked me warmly for the very genuine sympathy that I expressed to him; we passed two days more together, and I left him with regret.

I could not make him promise to write me.

"No," he answered, "I have stirred up the ashes on my hearth too much by relating you my life. The fire must all go out, forever. If I made a habit of touching it from time to time, I could no longer master it. I see plainly that you pity me; I should begin to pity myself; that must not be!"

I placed myself at his disposal for any service that I could render him, and left him my address. He never wrote to me, and did not even acknowledge the receipt of some books that he had requested me to send him.

Eighteen months had elapsed since my visit to Auvergne, and I was still inspector of finance; my duties had called me to Normandy, and I returned from Yvetot to Duclair, in a little hired calash, on a cold December evening.

The road was good, and, notwithstanding the very gloomy weather, I preferred to arrive at my lodging a little late than be forced to rise very early in the morning, the cold being the sharpest at daybreak.

I had been travelling an hour, when the weather softened beneath the influence of a very heavy snow. An hour later, the road was so covered with it that my driver, whose name was Thomas, and who was a somewhat indolent old man, had some difficulty in not carrying me across country. His hacks several times refused to advance, and at last they refused so effectually that we had to alight to disengage the wheels and take the beasts by the bridle;

but it was all in vain. We were stuck in a ditch. It was then that M. Thomas confessed that he was no longer sure of the way to Duclair, and that he believed we were on the one that led back to Caudebec. We were in the midst of woods, on a very deeply sunken road ; the violence of the snow-storm increased, and there was a great risk in remaining there. Not a carriage, not a cart, not a passer by to aid us and direct us.

I was just deciding to roll myself in my cloak, and sleep in the carriage, when M. Thomas told me that he recognized his whereabouts, and that we were in the woods between Jumiéges and Saint Vandrille. These two residences were too far apart to enable the exhausted horses to take us to either; but there was a château nearer, where he was well known, and where we should receive hospitality. I had pitied the poor man, who was as tired as his horses, and I promised him to watch them, while he went through the woods to seek assistance at the neighboring château.

It was very near, in reality, for at the end of quarter of an hour I saw him returning with a reinforcement of two men and a horse. They quickly extricated us, and one of the men, who appeared to be a farm-laborer, told me that we could not regain the road to Duclair in this bad weather. One could not see three steps before him.

"My master," added he, "would be very angry if I did not bring you to sup and sleep at the château."

"Who is your master, my friend?"

"It is Baron Lawrence," he replied.

"Who ?" cried I, "Baron Lawrence, the deputy ? "

"It is his château," replied the peasant, " which you would see from here, if one could see anything. But come, it does no good to stay there. The horses are in a sweat."

"Go on," I said, "I will follow you."

As the road was very narrow, I literally followed the carriage and the men, and I could address no further questions on the subject of Baron Lawrence ; but it was certainly the uncle of my friend the actor. There was but one Lawrence in the Chamber of Deputies, and I wondered at the destiny that was leading me to this potentate of the family. I resolved forthwith to see him, to acquaint him with his nephew's situation, to tell him all the good I thought of this young man, and to combat him if he undervalued him.

The snow, which continued to fall, did not suffer me to see the manor clearly. We seemed to pass through narrow courts, surrounded by lofty buildings. I ascended a broad flight of steps, and was admitted by a servant, who received me very politely, telling me that they were preparing my apartment, and that meanwhile I should find a good fire in the dining-room.

While speaking he relieved me of my snowy great-coat, and passed a bit of cloth over my boots. A great door was opened opposite, and I saw another domestic about to place savory dishes upon a richly appointed table. An immense buhl clock struck the hour of midnight.

"I suppose," said I to the servant, "that the Baron is in bed, and will not disturb himself for an unknown traveller whom this stormy night has brought to his house. Have the goodness to give him my card to-morrow, and if he will permit me to thank him — "

"The Baron has not gone to bed," returned the domestic; "it is his supper hour, and I will take him monsieur's card."

He ushered me into the dining-hall, and disappeared. The other domestic, engaged in serving supper, politely placed me a chair near the fire, threw an armful of pine-cones upon it, and resumed his occupations, without speaking.

I was not cold; I was in a perspiration. I regarded my surroundings. This great hall resembled the refectory of an ancient convent. On looking closer I assured myself that it was not a modern imitation, but a genuine Roman and monastic architecture, something like a branch of Jumiéges or Saint Vandrille, the two celebrated abbeys which once possessed all the surrounding country. Baron Lawrence had transformed the convent into a palace, even as Prince Klémenti. The adventures of the Bellamare troupe recurred to my memory, and I almost expected to see the Friar Ischion or the Commandant Nikanor enter, when the double door at the back of the room was opened, and a tall person, in crimson satin dressing-gown trimmed with fur, advanced to meet me with open arms. It was not Prince Klémenti; it was not Baron Lawrence; it was my friend Lawrence, — Lawrence in

person, a little stouter, but handsomer than ever.

I embraced him with joy. He had come to a reconciliation with his uncle, then; he was the heir presumptive of his title and his wealth!

"My uncle is dead," he replied. "He died without knowing me and without thinking of me; but he had forgotten to make his will, and, as I was his only relative — "

"Only? your father? — "

"My poor dear father! — dead likewise, dead of joy! struck with apoplexy when a notary came to tell him, without preparation, that we were rich. He did not understand that he had lost his brother. He saw only the brilliant lot that had fallen to me, the one hope, the one anxiety of his life; this desire had become more intense with the fear of my damnation. He threw himself into my arms, saying, 'You are a lord, you will never be an actor again! I can die!' and he died. You see, my friend, that this fortune costs me very dear! But we will talk at our leisure; you must be fatigued and chilled. Let us sup; I will keep you as long as possible afterward. I desire to see you, to renew our acquaintance, and resume my story to you; for since our meeting and our separation, I have not had an hour of confidential conversation."

When we were at table he sent away his servants.

"My friends," he said to them, "you know that I like to keep late hours, without making the others do so. Put within our reach whatever we shall require, be certain that nothing is lacking in my guest's apartment, and go to bed, if you desire."

"At what hour is it necessary to wake monsieur the Baron's guest?" asked the valet.

"You will let him sleep," replied Lawrence, "and you will cease to call me the Baron; I have already requested you not to give me a title that does not belong to me."

The servant left the room with a sigh.

"You see," said Lawrence, when we were alone, "nothing is wanting to my disguise, not even the valets of comedy. Those think themselves lowered by serving a man without title and without arrogance. They are great idiots who incommode me more than they assist me, and who, I hope, will leave me of themselves, when they see that I treat them like men."

"I believe, on the contrary," said I, "that they will, after a little, think themselves very fortunate to be treated so. Give them time to understand it."

"If they understand I will keep them, but I doubt if they become accustomed to the manners of a man who has no desire of personal attendance."

"Or you accustom yourself to being thus attended. You are more aristocratic in appearance and in manners, my dear Lawrence, than any *châtelain* that I have met."

"I play my rôle, dear friend! I know how one should be before the domestics of a good family. I know that, to be respected by them, it needs great kindness and great politeness; for they, also, are actors who

despise what they pretend to venerate; but do not deceive yourself, those that you see here are very vulgar strolling players. My uncle was a counterfeit grandee; at bottom he had all the absurdities of a parvenu who detests his origin. I have seen that in the attitude and habits of his people. Their vanity is of a third-rate order; when they have left me, I shall take better ones, and those will regard me as a truly superior man, because I shall play my part of aristocrat better than any aristocrat whatever. Is it not all fiction and comedy in this world? I do not know, for my part! I asked myself, on taking possession of this estate, if I could endure it for eight days. I did not so much fear being bored by it, as appearing out of place and feeling ridiculous in it; but, when I saw how easy it was to impose upon people in society by a borrowed ease and dignity, I perceived that my old theatrical profession was an excellent education, and that they ought to give a similar one to young men of family."

Lawrence uttered several other paradoxes in a tone of raillery that was not mirthful. He affected a little too much disdain for his new station.

"Come," I said, "do not act a part with a man to whom you have unveiled the inmost recesses of your heart and conscience. It is impossible that you are not happier here than in your village. I put aside your father's death which was inevitable, according to the laws of nature; this sorrow is not so connected with your inheritance that it should prevent you from appreciating its advantages."

"Pardon me," he replied, "that sorrow and this fortune are closely connected. I told you frankly formerly, I tell you to-day, with the same sincerity, I am a born actor. I had not the talent, but I have kept the passion for it. I have a need to be greater than nature. I have to pose in my own eyes, to forget the man that I am, and ascend, by imagination, above my own individuality. All the difference between the professional actor and myself is that he requires the public, while, as for me, never having much impressed it, I do without it very well; but my chimera is necessary to me; it has sustained me, it has made me accomplish great sacrifices. I know that I am good and honorable; that is not sufficient for me; nature made me so; I aspire, incessantly, to be sublime in my own eyes, and to be so by the act of my will. In short, virtue is my rôle, and I wish to play no other. I know that I shall always play it, or I should take a disgust and aversion to myself. You do not understand that, you take me for a madman? You do not deceive yourself; I am one, but my madness is noble, and, since I must have one, do not seek to deprive me of that. I was truly stoical in my village, for everybody there believed me happy, and I was only so at rare moments, when I could say to myself, 'You have succeeded in being great.' The life of my father, his security, which was my work, was the reason of my sacrifice. I had reached the point when I no longer regretted the past.

At present, what have I to do here that is worthy of me? Have fine manners, express myself more correctly, be more literary than the greater part of the gentlemen who observe and sound me, to know if they may accept me as one of their 'set'? It is really too easy, and it is not an ideal of which I feel very desirous."

I asked him if they were aware, in his new province, that he had been an actor.

"They had heard of it; they repeated it; they were not sure of it, although they had seen formerly upon the stage at Rouen a tall, slender young man who resembled me much, and who bore upon the poster the same name as the Baron. They could not then suppose that I was his relative. He was not accustomed to do the honors for his plebeian connections. When I presented myself as his heir, they questioned my people, who knew nothing and denied indignantly. They questioned me more adroitly, and I hastened to tell the truth with so much boldness and pride, that they hastened to reply that I 'was none the worse for that.' A man who has a hundred thousand francs a year, my dear friend, is not a cipher in the provinces; he is a useful or injurious power, and all who surround him have more or less need of him. I perceived at once that I must either realize my capital and leave the country, or assume the appearance of cleverness. That was part of my monomania, and I played the man of accomplishments, without exerting myself in the least."

"Cease this strain of irony toward

yourself, my dear Lawrence. You were very frank in relating me your life; be so still. You are a man of very intelligent mind, so you are really clever. You wish to appear what you are, it is your right; I will say more, it is your duty. I see nothing in you which savors of the actor, unless it is this affectation of sneering at the social station where destiny places you, which I begin to understand. The man who has subjected his whole being, intellect, face, accent, heart, and feeling to the judgment of a public, often unjust and cruel, has certainly suffered much from this direct contact, and his pride necessarily revolts at the idea that, for a few sous paid at the door, any clown buys the right to humiliate him. I confess that, before knowing you, I had a great scorn for actors. I pardoned only those whose real talent has the right to brave and the power to vanquish all. I felt a sort of disgust for those who were mediocre, and I overcame this disgust only by the compassion with which their distress inspired me, the difficulty of living in this world, the lack of early education, the obstacles to work in modern society. It is this ever-increasing difficulty of finding work, when one is not remarkably endowed, which combats and destroys the prejudice against actors more than all the philosophical arguments; for, at bottom, this prejudice is not without foundation. To present one's self to the public, painted and attired like a buffoon or a hero, that is, like a man who expects to excite the laughter or the tears of a multitude, requires a boldness which

is courage or audacity; and whoever pays has surely a right to cry to him, 'Go to! you are not fine or you are not funny!' Ah well, my dear Lawrence, you say that you were passable, and that was all. So you suffered from not being in the first rank, and sought to console yourself by saying to yourself, with reason, that, in you, the man was superior to the artist; and now that you recall the coldness of the people from the other side of the footlights, you unconsciously cherish a bitterness against them. You force yourself to treat them haughtily, as they treated you, when you belonged to them. They did not find you enough of an actor, and you desire to tell them that their existence is likewise a play to them, that it is bad, and they perform it badly. That is a commonplace which proves nothing, for all is, in reality, frightfully serious, in the drama of the world, and in the world of the drama. Forget, then, this little bitterness. Accept freely your return to liberty and social action. You have a great excuse, an excuse that you have candidly confessed to me, *love*, which is the grand absolution of youth. This love is forgotten, I suppose; if not, it is now able to conquer everything, I suppose again. In any case, you have nothing to blush for in the past; and that is why you ought to greet the world, not like a repentant or defiant fugitive, but like a traveller, who has profited by his experience to judge all things impartially, and who returns home to reflect and act like a philosopher."

Lawrence heard my little sermon through, without interrupting it; and as he had still a child's heart in a manly breast, he extended both hands to me with emotion.

"You are right," he said; "I feel that you are right, and that you do me good. Ah! if I had a friend near me! I have such need of one, and I am so lonely! Stay, my friend, my whole life is a giddiness, and I am not twenty-eight! I have passed through existences so different, that I no longer really know who I am. All is adventure and romance in this agitated life. There was truly cause to be a little mad. Without you, I should have become utterly so, for, when you met me in a public-house, I was in a fair way to become a village good-for-nothing, perhaps a wretched drunkard, dreaming of suicide in the fumes of the blue wine. Thanks to you, I regained the mastery over myself; but the exaltation increased, and it was time to end it. My poor father, forgive me what I say!"

A tear trembled on his eyelashes; he mechanically poured himself a second glass of malmsey. He turned it out, and as I looked at him he said, "I no longer drink, unless through inadvertency, without knowing what I do. If I remember, you see, I abstain."

"Still, you have your supper at this hour every evening?"

"Yes, a habit of the actor, who loves to turn night into day."

"In the village, however—"

"In the village, I worked all day like an ox, but on Saturday, Sunday, and Monday I did like the others, and those days I did not go to bed. What would you have,—*ennui?* Still

I was a good workman. Already there has ceased to be a trace of it. See! I have white hands, as handsome hands as when I played the lover's rôle. It does not follow that I enjoy myself. Ah! my friend, I speak to you frankly, do not take this for an affectation. I am bored enough to bite off my tongue; I am bored to death."

"Were you not able to create serious occupations for yourself again?"

"Serious! Tell me, then, what there is serious in the life of a newly made millionnaire, who is still a stranger in the sphere of practical people. Shall I never be practical, myself? Can I be so? Hear the recital of my three months of country life in this château; but we have remained long enough at table. Come into my room, we shall be more comfortable there."

He took up a silver-gilt candlestick, exquisitely wrought, and after having conducted me through a splendid drawing-room, an immense billiard-saloon, and a marvellous boudoir, he ushered me into a sleeping-room, where I cried out directly, "The blue room!"

"What!" he said, smiling, "you recollect my story well enough, my brief description struck you sufficiently for you to recognize things you have never seen!"

"My dear friend, your story produced such an impression on me that I amused myself by writing it out in my spare moments, changing all the names. I will read it to you, and if my reminiscences lack exactness, if I have altered the coloring, you will correct, you will rectify, you will change; I will leave you the manuscript."

He told me that it would give him the greatest pleasure.

"This is, then," I resumed, "the famous blue chamber?"

"It is as exact a copy as my own memory afforded me."

"You are then once more enamored of the beautiful unknown?"

"My friend, the beautiful unknown is dead; all is dead in the romance of my life."

"But the famous troupe, Bellamare, Léon, Moranbois,—and she whom I dare not name?"

"They are all dead to me. Absent in America, I know not where; Impéria, having lost her father, accompanied them to Canada, where they were still, six months ago. Bellamare wrote me that he should be in a position, on his return, to refund my money. Every one was well. Let us not speak of them; it troubles me somewhat, and I am, perhaps, on the way to forget—"

"Heaven grant it! It is what I desire above all things for you; but this blue room, it is a souvenir that you have wished, that you wish to preserve?"

"Yes; when I learned that my unknown lived no longer, her memory regained possession of my heart, and, like the grown-up child that I am, I wished to raise this familiar monument to her memory. You remember that this blue chamber was no more hers than the Renaissance house which I entered by mistake. This charming dwelling, rendered poetical for me by a gracious and kindly apparition, was, none the less, the only frame wherein I could evoke her veiled image. I have copied the room as well as I was able; only, as this is larger, I could add to it good sofas where we will smoke good cigars."

I asked him how and from whom he had learned the death of his unknown.

"I will tell you directly," he responded. "It is necessary to proceed in order. I resume my story. It will be but a short chapter to add to the romance that you have taken the trouble to write out."

III.

After my poor father's funeral I departed for Normandy, in the frame of mind belonging to a man who travels in quest of change to distract himself from a profound sorrow, in no wise with the intoxication of a poor wretch who wins in a lottery and goes to receive his capital. Of my first and only visit to my uncle I had retained a very disagreeable impression. He had not received me cordially, you remember, since you remember everything; and his housekeeper had looked askance at me. I found the manor as he had left it, namely, in a very good state of repair. The old bachelor was an orderly man; there was not a slate missing from his roof, nor a stone from his walls; but the interior decoration was in a detestable style. There was gilding everywhere, taste nowhere. As everything had been put under seal, and as, until his last hour, he had been domineering and suspicious, his housekeeper, who did not govern him as much as I had supposed, had been unable to plunder freely. I found, beside a splendid estate, very productive farm-rents, affairs in very good order, and large sums in the bank. I discharged the housekeeper, begging her to carry off three fourths of the rich and hideous furniture, and, yielding to an artist's fancy, an irresistible desire to establish a harmony in every portion of this monument of a bygone age, I passed all my time in installing myself with taste, with learning, with judgment; in short, exercising my ingenuity to combine comfort with archæology. You will see this to-morrow by daylight; I have succeeded tolerably well, I think, and it will be better when it is all finished. Only, I am afraid, when I have nothing more to do in my house, that I shall not be able to remain in it; for, if I pause for a moment, I yawn and wish to weep. I was not long in perceiving that, if I desired to spare myself much annoyance and distrust, I must reply politely to the attentions that were bestowed on me. I had taken a list of my uncle's friends and acquaintances; I had sent out invitations in my name, since I was the only representative of the family. I received many cards, and even those of the greatest "big-wigs." I ventured to visit them. I was received with more curiosity than cordiality; but it appears that I speedily triumphed over all prejudices. They thought I had much depth and a perfect style. They knew that I had conducted affairs, on taking posses-

sion, in a princely manner. All my visits were returned. They found me occupied in patching up my old walls, and realized that I was not an ignorant bourgeois. My taste and my expenditures established me as a connoisseur and artist, my seclusion ended by making me appear a man of serious disposition. They had imagined I should frequent bad company. What company could I keep? That of actors? I should not know where to find one of those whom I had known, wandering about the world. Workmen of my village? Unless I gave them a pension, I could not take them from their labor.

They did not make allowance for the extraordinary isolation into which an exceptional destiny had thrown me; they believed that I voluntarily abstained from good-fellowship and nocturnal revelry. They were infinitely obliged to me for it. They invited me to appear in the society of the place. I replied that the recent death of my father rendered me still too sad and too little social. They admired me for having loved my father! The young men, my neighbors, invited me to join their field sports. I promised to take part in them, when I had finished my installation labors. They were astonished, on leaving for Paris in the beginning of the winter, that I had no regret in remaining behind; they would have presented me in the best society. I did not wish to appear eccentric; I promised to become later a man of the world. But my resolution is quite taken, my dear friend. I have already seen the most of these people. Their existence will never be mine. They are nearly all empty. Those who seem to possess intelligence and information have contracted, in their prosperous circumstances, habits of idleness that would drive me mad. Those who serve the government are machines. Those who have independence of thought do not use their mental energy, or they abuse it. All take seriously this thing, without cohesion and without object, that they call the world, and in which I find nothing that has a serious meaning. No, no; once more, do not think that my distrust arises from a foregone conclusion; on the contrary, I seek with anxiety the luminous point in it that could attract and impassion me. I see there only a confused swarm of little things, insignificant, incomplete, unfinished. I have as yet seen only the rehearsals of the play that they perform there. Ah well, this play is desultory, incomprehensible, devoid of interest, passion, grandeur, or gayety. The actors whom I have been able to study are incapable of disentangling it; for those who have talent are scornful or *blasé*, or they feel that their rôles are unachievable and play them coldly. I have been nourished, myself, on noble tragedies and fine dramas. The worst production of art has, moreover, some plan and seeks to prove something; an evening in society seems to have no object save to kill time. What would you have a man do there, accustomed before the public to order his gestures, time his entrances, not say a useless word, not take a random step? To represent an action is to act from logic and reason;

to utter nothings forgotten as soon as said, to listen to idle discussions that good taste forbids even to be deep, is to evince good breeding and knowledge of the world; but it is doing nothing at all, and I am unable to resign myself forever to doing nothing.

The moral of this is not that an actor is too superior to reality to identify himself with it; do not attribute such a boast to me; but understand, then, that any artist whatever converts reality into a mould that his personality occupies and fills. Where his imprint does not mark, he ceases to live; he petrifies. I need to be, not that they may see that I am, but in order to feel that I exist. For the moment, I am archæologist, antiquarian, numismatologist; later, I shall be, perhaps, naturalist, or painter, or chronicler, or novelist, or agriculturist, who can tell? I must always have a passion, a task, an interest; but I shall never be deputy, or prefect, or sportsman, or diplomat, or politician, or treasurer; nothing, in short, that constitutes at the present day what is called a practical man. I shall see if this house that I create inspires me with some idea; if not, I shall leave it and go abroad. But I fear solitude in travelling, as I fear idleness in sedentary life. What is necessary to me, what belongs to my age, what my heart demands, at the same time that it dreads is love, is family life. I should wish to be married, for I shall never know how to bring myself to marry. Still, the thought has occurred to me several times, since knowing my neighbor, and it is time that I tell you of my neighbor.

Her name is Jeanne, and she has wavy brown hair. Those are her only defects; for they are her sole points of resemblance to Impéria, whose name, as you remember, is Jane de Valclos; and I should have preferred to love a woman who recalled in no respect the one for whom I have suffered so much. For the rest, the contrast is complete. She is tall and beautiful; the other was small and pretty. She has not the ringing voice or the clear utterance of an actress. Hers is a sweet voice, a little indistinct and muffled, which caresses and does not thrill; an utterance which glides on without emphasis, and lays stress only on what is deeply felt. I should say, generally, of this woman, that she is an instrument furnished with those silken strings which have not resonance enough for the orchestra of an opera, but which give out more melody and sweetness in *musica di camera*.

She is tall and beautiful, I told you, and I will add that she is a little awkward, which pleases me infinitely. She would not know how to take three steps upon a stage, without hitting something. This is due to a short-sightedness, which does not allow her to see the outlines of objects without a glass. As for me, the source of instinct and of taste lies in the sense of sight. Those whose extended vision embraces all things are plastic; on the other hand, those who need to look closely are specialists. My neighbor's specialty is domestic life, a little activity that is not exercised abroad, but which is ingenious and incessant, a watchful and continual solicitude, delicate and inexhaustible for those whose care she undertakes. She is just the opposite of me, who know how to exercise devotion by a great act of resolution, but who, returned to myself, can no longer see anything, except through myself. But she forgets herself; she would take any stamp one chose to give her; she would know how to be *another*, to see with his eyes, to breathe with his lungs, to identify herself with him and disappear.

You see she is the ideal of a companion, a friend, a wife. Add to this that she is free, a widow, and without children. She is very nearly my own age. She is rich enough to have no care for my fortune, and her birth is the same as mine, her grandfather was a peasant. She has been in society, but was never fond of it. She intends to leave it entirely, having met no one who made her desire to marry again. She learned that the abbey of Saint Vandrille was to let for a tolerably moderate sum; and as she has sufficient taste and knowledge to love the preservation of beautiful things, she came to pass some months in its vicinity, to ascertain if the climate would agree with her health, and if the surrounding country would secure her the sort of tranquil and retired life for which she longs. The cottage she has rented joins my park, and we meet once or twice a week; we might meet every day; the obstacle, alas! is on my side, my faintheartedness, my dwelling on the past, my fear of no longer knowing how to love, despite the need of love that is consuming me.

I must tell you how we became acquainted. It was the most prosaic way in the world. I had been passing two days at Fécamp in search of a head-workman for the purpose of repairing some admirable old wainscots, banished to the loft by my predecessor. Returning quite late at night, I slept late in the morning, and I saw, from my window, this beautiful and charming woman, in close conversation with the wood-carver, who was beginning on his work in the open air, opposite the hall on the ground-floor. She was so simply dressed, that it needed attentive observation to recognize in her a woman of certain rank in the hierarchy of gentlewomen. I descended to the apartment that he was engaged in decorating; and when I saw the boot, the glove, and the cuff, I doubted no longer. It was a Parisian lady and a most refined person. I went out into the court; I saluted her on passing, and was not going to interrupt her investigation, when she approached me with a mixture of good-breeding and timidity which lent a great charm to her act.

"I ought," she said, "to beg pardon of the master of Bertheville (that is the name of my abbey) for the freedom with which I have entered the open gates of his domain."

"Pardon!" I replied, "when I should thank you for it!"

"That is very kind," she replied, with a playful simplicity that did not prevent her from coloring a little; "but I will not trespass on it. I will withdraw, and, knowing that you are here, of which I was not yet aware, I will not permit myself again —"

"I will take my departure again, forthwith, if it interferes with your examining my work."

"I have finished. I came to ask directions on my own account."

I offered to give her what information lay in my power as proprietor, and she saw that my manner was perfectly serious and proper. She did not scruple to tell me that she had desired Saint Vandrille, but that she was dismayed by the expenditure necessary to render this ruin habitable. She had wished to learn from my head-workman the price of his work. There was at Saint Vandrille a very fine wainscot of this kind which also required a restoration.

I had already seen Saint Vandrille, but without making any calculation of its improvement. I proposed to go there that same day, and make a little study, accompanied with a rough estimate of the expense. She accepted my offer, thanking me warmly, but telling me that she would send for my study, and urging me not to bring it to her.

When she left me, I was a little bewildered by her beauty and her air of frankness; I recovered myself directly. I laughed at myself for my excessive civility, for I was about to lose a day and give myself considerable trouble for a person who did not care to see me again; but I had promised, and two hours later I was at Saint Vandrille. I found my beautiful neighbor there, who came and thanked me for my promptness.

In the mean time I had made inquiries about her. I learned that her name was Madame de Valdère; that she usually resided in Paris; that she had just hired a house close by me; that she lived absolutely alone with an old governess, a cook, and a servant, not knowing, and not yet wishing to know, any one in the neighborhood, passing her mornings in walking, and her evenings in embroidering or reading.

Saint Vandrille is, like Jumiéges, a vast ruin in a small enclosure. You know Jumiéges, doubtless. If you do not, figure to yourself the church of Saint Sulpice ruined and laid open in the midst of a pretty English garden, whose sanded alleys wind through fine grass-plots under open arches tapestried with ivy and garlanded with wild plants. The two monumental church towers rear their skeletons, white as old bones against the beautiful Norman sky, so rich in color when the sun pierces its mists. Countless birds of prey circle incessantly around these open turrets, whose carved border protects their nests, and send forth loud hoarse cries. Below the great walls of the uncovered nave grow magnificent trees and graceful bushes. In a remnant of the old buildings for religious service, the present owner, a man of taste and learning, has arranged himself a dwelling, still very large, and decorated in the best style. From fragments found in the ruins, he has made an interesting museum. It is a habitation at once stern, comfortable, and charming, fronting a splendid scenery enlivened and perfumed by a delightful vegetation well ordered in its picturesque arrangement.

In examining Saint Vandrille, we spoke only of Jumiéges, whose adaptation was a masterpiece in my eyes, and might serve as a model for Madame de Valdère.

"I realize perfectly," she said to me, "that the acquisition of these historical monuments creates serious duties. To restore them is only in the power of princely fortunes, and I do not quite see where would be the benefit to art and science which have already sufficient archaeological specimens still standing. Besides, I attach no value to what is almost entirely made over, with new materials and by hands which no longer possess the individuality of the past. When a ruin is truly a ruin, one should leave it its relative beauty, its lofty air of desertion, its marriage with the ivy that encroaches on it, and the solemnity of its associations. To preserve it from brutal devastation, to frame it with verdure and with flowers, is all one can and ought to do, and this part of my mission I should fulfil well enough, I believe; I love gardens and I possess a little knowledge of them; but the appropriation of my residence to this exacting neighborhood is what disquiets me; there is a species of slavery in this sort of property that terrifies me. One has no right to refuse admittance to amateurs, or even to the idle and indifferent. Hence one ceases to be at home; and what shall I do, I who am so fond of solitude, if I cannot walk among my ruins, without encountering there at every step English tourists or photographers ? If we were close by Paris, one would have special days and hours to devote to the public ; but here, has one a right to deny people who have come thirty or forty leagues to see a ruin of which you are, in reality, only the guardian or *ciccrone ?*"

To that I had nothing to reply. I knew by what thoughtless demands, by what rude returns, the inexhaustible civility of our neighbor of Jumiéges was too often repaid. I advised Madame de Valdère to build herself a châlet in the midst of the woods, and to think no more of Saint Vandrille.

I ought to have rested on this wise conclusion, to have abandoned my valuation, and taken leave of her ; but the passion for archæology led me away. The church of Saint-Vandrille is finer and in many places better preserved than that of Jumiéges. The adjacent buildings are ugly and inconvenient ; but there is a quadrangular garden which descends in terraces above smiling meadows ; and this monastic garden, designed in ancient style, was a great temptation for my dreams of conscientious decoration. There was also an immense chapter-house there, quite entire, and completely surrounded by elegant arcades. From a great gallery which communicates with the refectory one penetrates into the vast structure. I saw myself again in the chapter-house of Saint Clément. I recalled the magisterial conference of the prince with his vassals, the hurried and mournful funeral of Marco ; then, my hallucination following its bent, I believed I stood once more in the immense library where we had acted tragedy before the chiefs of Montenegro. Again I saw Impéria singing and miming the *Marseillaise*, and, in a confusion of phantoms and fictions, Lambesq roaring the furies of Orestes, while I declaimed Polyeucte. The kind and pleasant face of Bellamare appeared to me from behind the scenes, whence the hollow voice of Moranbois gave us the cue. Tears sprang to my eyes, a nervous laugh choked me, and I cried involuntarily, " Ah ! what a fine theatre ! "

Madame de Valdère regarded me with emotion ; she doubtless thought that I was mad ; she grew pale and trembling.

I thought I must, to reassure her, make her the declaration that I am wont to throw at those who look at me with distrust and curiosity.

" I have been an actor," I said to her, forcing a smile.

" I know it well," she answered, still agitated. " I believe I am acquainted with your whole history. Do not be surprised at it, Monsieur Lawrence. I had a pretty little Renaissance house at Blois, No. 25, in a certain street where there were lindens and nightingales. There occurred in this house a singular adventure, of which you were the hero. The heroine, who went there without my knowledge or permission, although she was a friend of mine, confessed all to me afterwards. Poor woman, she died with this memory ! "

" Died ! " cried I. " Then I shall never see her ! "

" So much the better for her, since you would not have loved her ! "

I saw that Madame de Valdère

knew all. I pressed her with questions; she evaded them; this memory was painful to her, and she was in no wise disposed to betray the secret of her friend. I should never know her name, nor anything which would enable me to trace her in a past sealed up, buried irrevocably.

"You can at least," I said, "tell me of the feeling that she had for me. Was it serious?"

"Very serious, very deep, very lasting; you had not thought it?"

"No, and I probably missed happiness through distrust of happiness; but did she suffer from this love? Was it the cause —"

"Of her premature death? No. She had preserved her hope, or had recovered it, when she learned that you had left the stage. Perhaps she was about to attempt to regain your affections, when she died in consequence of an accident,—her ball-dress caught fire. She suffered greatly; she has been dead for two years. Let us talk no more of her, I beg of you; it gives me great pain."

"It pains me also," I replied, "and yet I wish to speak of her! Have a little courage, through pity for me."

She answered kindly that she sympathized with my regret, if it was real; but could it be? Should I not continue to scorn, beyond the tomb, a woman whom I had scorned when living? Was I disposed to listen with respect to what I might be told concerning her?

I assured her that I was.

"That is not sufficient," replied Madame de Valdère. "I wish to know your inmost feelings in this respect. Relate me your adventure frankly, from your point of view. Tell me the judgment that you passed upon my friend, and all the reasons that led you to write that you adored her, to forget her afterward, and to return to the beautiful Impéria."

I faithfully related to her all that I have told you, without omitting anything. I confessed that there was, perhaps, a certain pique in my first impulse toward the unknown, and a second pique in my silence when she had doubted me.

"I was sincere," I told her; "I had loved Impéria, but I threw myself into a new love courageously, loyally, ardently. Your friend might have saved me; she was unwilling. I should never have seen Impéria again. I should have forgotten her without an afterthought or a regret. Nothing was easier for me at that time. The unknown showed herself jealous in a haughty way, whose cold generosity humiliated me profoundly. I feared a person exacting to the point of making it a crime in me to have loved another before knowing her, and mistress of herself to the point of concealing her disdain beneath benefits. I should have preferred an open jealousy; I should have found agitated words, heartfelt oaths, to reassure her. I foresaw terrible struggles, an invincible bitterness gathered in her heart. I was a craven in my pride. I renounced her! And then her position and mine were too unequal! Now, I should no longer be so timid and so easily offended. I should not fear to seem ambitious to her, and I should know how to conquer her distrust; but she exists no longer; it was my destiny to be unfortunate in love. She did not know how much I might have loved her; and I was rejected by Impéria, as if Heaven had wished to punish me for not having caught at happiness when it was offered me."

"Yes," replied Madame de Valdère, "in that respect you were very culpable toward yourself, and you cruelly misunderstood a woman as loyal and as sincere as yourself. My friend wrote in good faith when she offered you her assistance with Impéria. She was neither distrustful nor haughty. She was weighed down with grief; she sacrificed herself. She was not perfect, but she had the utter candor of romantic souls; in feeling a dread of her character, you committed, permit me to say, the greatest blunder that a man of judgment could commit. She possessed a gentleness that might degenerate into weakness, and you could have governed like a child this woman whom you fancied terrible."

"I was a child, myself," I answered, "and I was well punished for it!"

"Doubtless, since you recovered your love for Impéria, and that love became an incurable malady."

"What do you know of it?" I exclaimed.

"I saw it at once, when you cried, 'There would be a fine theatre!' All your past of illusions, all your future of regrets, were written in your eyes; you will never console yourself!"

It seemed to me like a direct reproach, for the eyes of this beautiful woman were moist and shining. I caught her hand, without quite knowing what I did.

"Let us talk no more of either Impéria or the unknown," I said. "There has ceased to be a past for me; why should there not be a future?"

I perceived, to my surprise, that I was making her a declaration, and I made haste to add: "Let us talk of Saint Vandrille."

I offered her my arm to descend to the wild and deserted garden, and we did not talk of Saint Vandrille. We still returned to the unknown; and I thought I could perceive that, by dint of talking of me and describing me to Madame de Valdère, she had excited in her a great curiosity to see me, perhaps a stronger interest than curiosity. My neighbor appeared to me, if not as adventurous as her friend, at least as romantic; and I began to feel that it would be very easy to fall in love with her, if I was encouraged ever so little.

I was not, and I became more enamored. I had not dared to ask her to receive me; she secluded herself so completely for some days, that I prowled in vain about her dwelling without perceiving her. It was then that the fancy occurred to me to transform my uncle's sleeping-room into a study, and to install my Penates in the square pavilion, which should become the blue chamber of Blois. From the moment that I knew the veritable designer of this pretty apartment, it gained a double interest for me, and I began to work at it from memory, with much enthusiasm. When, at the end of several days, it began to resemble the original, I wrote to Madame de Valdère to beg her to give me some information and advice upon my premises. I had been so courteous to her, that she thought she could not refuse me. She came, was greatly surprised, greatly touched, even, by my sentimental fancy, and declared that my recollections were very faithful. She permitted me, then, to visit her, and showed me two letters to the unknown that the latter, on dying, had confided to her, telling her to burn them after she had read them.

" Why have you not done so? " I asked her.

" I don't know," she answered ; " I have always dreamed that I should meet you somewhere, and could return them to you."

Still, she did not return them, and I had no motive to reclaim them. I asked her if she had not a portrait of her friend.

" No," she said, " and if I had one, I should not show it to you."

" Why ? Her distrust continued ; she forbade you, — so be it ! I will love no more in the past; I have had enough of it ; I have been unhappy enough to have expiated everything. I have a right to forget my long martyrdom."

" Still, the blue chamber ? "

" The blue chamber, it is you," I answered. " It is you, designer and occupant of this room, that in this room I loved in fancy, before the apparition of your friend."

" Then that is likewise the past ? "

" Why should it not be the present ? "

She reproached me for coming to her house to pay her empty compliments.

It was bad taste, I confessed, but what could she expect of a former stage-lover ?

" Hush," said she, " you slander yourself ! I know you very well ; my friend had received letters enough from M. Bellamare to appreciate you'; and I, who read those letters, know what you are. Do not hope to make me doubt."

" What am I, according to you ? "

" A serious and delicate man, who will never lightly make love to a woman he esteems ; a man who, for three years, concealed his affection from Impéria, because he respected her. Hence, a woman who respects herself and who knows that would not willingly accept flattery from you ; confess it."

I did not then make love to Madame de Valdère; I do not now ; but I see her often, and I love her. It seems to me that she loves me also. Perhaps I am a coxcomb ; perhaps she has only friendship for me, like Impéria ! It is, perhaps, my destiny to inspire friendship. It is sweet, it is pure, it is charming, but it is not sufficient. I begin to be irritated by this confidence in my loyalty, which is not as real as it appears, since it costs me a struggle. And this is where I am. A lover, timid and distrustful, impatient and fearful, because — because — must I tell you all ? — I have as much fear of being loved as of not being loved. I see that I have to do with a thoroughly virtuous woman, who would not understand a transient love, when she can belong to me forever. I aspire to the happiness of possessing such a wife, and loving her as I know that I am capable of loving. It only remains for me to give her this confidence by expressing a true passion to her; and there I have remained, for nearly two months, like a scholar, who fears to guess and who fears not to guess. Why, you will ask me —

"Yes," cried I, "why, say why, my dear Lawrence! Confess yourself entirely."

"Ah heavens," replied he, rising, and walking agitatedly about the blue chamber, "because I have contracted in my wandering life a very serious chronic malady; the unattainable desire, the fancy for the impossible, weariness of the real, the ideal without definite object, the thirst for what is not and cannot be! What I dreamed of at twenty I dream of still. What fled from my grasp I seek still in the empty air."

"The artist's glory! is it that?"

"Perhaps! I had, unconsciously, some unsatisfied ambition. I thought myself modest, because I wished to be so; but my wounded vanity has preyed upon me, like those diseases that you do not perceive and that kill you. Yes, it must be that! I could have wished to be a great artist, and I am only an intelligent critic. I am too cultivated, too logical, too philosophic, too reflective; I have not been inspired. I shall do very well a little of everything. I shall be a master in nothing. It is a torture to comprehend the beautiful, to have analyzed it, to know in what it consists, how it unfolds, develops, and manifests itself, and not be able to produce it from one's self. It is like love, you see! you feel it, you touch it, you think to seize it; it escapes you, it flees you. You stand before the memory of an ardent dream and of a cold deception!"

"Impéria!" I said, "it is Impéria! You think of her still!"

"Imperia insensible, and my ambition disappointed, it is all one," he answered. "These two first elements of vitality are the starting-point of my life. I wasted the three best years of my youth in seeing them elude me day by day, hour by hour. Perhaps I shall gain preferable blessings; but what I shall not recover is my boy's heart, my obstinate hope, my blind confidence, my poet aspirations, my days of carelessness, and my days of fever. All that is over, over! I am a grown man, and I love a grown woman. I am excellent; she is adorable; we could be very happy. I am rich as a nabob and lodged like a prince. From a straw-filled pallet I pass to a bed of gold and silk. I can gratify all my whims; get drunk on wine bottled these hundred years; have a harem better established and better concealed than that of Prince Klémènti. Still, better than he, I can have a theatre, a hired troupe; my uncle made me a grant of one hundred thousand francs like that of the Odéon! I shall have art for my money, as I have poetry by right of inheritance; a beautiful nature, where I prune and plant to my liking. See, is it not a romantic site?" added he, drawing aside the heavy curtain from the window, and showing me the landscape through the clear glass, frost-diamonded at the edge. "Look out! I do not like blinds. Nothing is sweeter than to look from one's fireside at the white frost without. The snow falls now only in light flakes, that the moon softly silvers. Farther on, below my park, the Seine, broad as an arm of the sea, flows peaceful and mighty. Those tall black cedars that frame the background let the masses of snow that drape their branches glide noiselessly upon the snow that drapes their feet. It is a beautiful scene, deliciously lighted! It is grand and solemn; it is mute as a churchyard, it is dead as I!—O Impéria!"

As he uttered this name, in an agonized voice that made the Loves of Saxony porcelain and the Bohemian glasses vibrate on the consoles, he stamped his foot like a necromancer who summons a rebellious spirit; all vibrated afresh, and all grew still again. He struck a blow that shivered to atoms a whole *étagère*, loaded with precious trifles. Then he began to laugh, saying with a bitter coolness, "Pay no attention; I often need to break something!"

"Lawrence, my dear Lawrence," I answered, "your malady is more serious than I thought. It is not an affectation, I see. You suffer much, and you are curing it in the wrong way. You must quit this solitude, you must travel, but with a companion. You must marry Madame de Valdère, and depart with her."

"If it concerned only myself," he replied, "I should not hesitate, for she pleases me, and I am sure that she is tender and devoted; but if I did not render her happy, if my sad-ness and my irregularities should afflict and distress her! At present she longs only to cure me of the past. I have ceased to conceal anything from her; she requires it. All that I tell you she hears; all that I let you see she sees; all that I suffer she knows. She questions me, she studies me, she makes me relate all the details of my past and present life. She is interested in it; she pities, consoles, chides, and pardons me. She is an angelic friend; she thinks she cures me, and I submit; and I imagine that she cures me, and I feel that she calms me. She is not too much disturbed by my relapses. She has an unheard-of patience! Ah well, yes, she is necessary to me, and I could no longer do without the balm she instils into my wounds. But I fear lest my love may be selfish, odious perhaps! For if they came to knock at my door, saying, 'Bellamare is below with Impéria; they have come for you to play at Caudebec or Yvetot,' I feel that I should rush down like a madman, that I should leap with tears of joy into their carriage, and that I should go with them to the end of the world. With this madness in my brain, would you have me swear to a loving woman to live only for her? What would be her humiliation and despair to have brooded so tenderly over this tame dove's egg, whence should escape a wild pigeon! No, I am not yet ready for marriage; you must not bid me hasten. I must have time to bury myself, and come to life again, if the thing is possible!"

He was right. We separated at three o'clock in the morning; I must absolutely leave at seven; but I promised him to despatch my affairs, and return to pass a week with him.

I had been at Duclair for two days, and I was breakfasting alone at the hotel table, not having been able to reach it at the accustomed hour, when I saw a man enter who was still young, that is to say, not very young, and not very handsome, that is, quite ugly, but whose salutation, glance, and smile prepossessed me in his favor. He seated himself opposite me, and ate hastily, without seeming to notice what they brought him, consulting a note-book meanwhile. I took him for a commercial traveller. Something at once lively, facetious, and kindly about him made me wish that he might address me; but he appeared too well bred to begin the conversation at random, and I resolved to anticipate him, by asking, what I knew very well, at what hour the steamer passed for Havre.

"I believe," he answered, "that it passes at two o'clock."

These few words were like a flash of light to me; he spoke through his nose! A vague revelation was already occurring to me, unconsciously. I wished to ask him his name, when I saw him draw up an inkstand, and write the address on a letter that he had taken from his pocket. I thoughtlessly cast my eyes upon this letter, and I read there, " For Monsieur Pierre Lawrence, Arvers."

"Permit me," I said to him. " By some unaccountable absence of mind, I have just looked at the name you are writing, and I believe I ought to give you a direction. Lawrence is no longer at Arvers."

He regarded me with a piercing glance, raising his eyes without lifting his head; and having assured himself that he had never seen me, but that I had an honest face, he requested me to be so kind as to give him Lawrence's new address.

"They call him Baron Lawrence here, but he does not like to have them give him this title, which he has not inherited in a direct line. He lives at his château, the château of his late uncle, at some hours' distance from here."

" He has inherited then ? "

"Effectually ; he has one hundred thousand francs a year."

" How he will laugh at my letter ! No matter ; have the goodness to tell me the name of the château."

" Bertheville."

" Ah ! true, I remember," said the man, gayly, with a broad smile. "What a stroke of luck ! That dear boy ! so he is rich and happy ! He well deserved it ! "

" He is not perhaps so happy as you think, Monsieur Bellamare."

" Ah ! so you know me then ? "

" You see I do ! "

" And him ? "

" He is my friend."

" Oh ! then — I know that you are inspector of finance, they told me so at this inn — you will have the goodness to take charge of that, a note of five thousand francs that I have owed him for some years. I know that he will dispense with the interest."

" And with the amount also. I assure you that he will not receive it ! No matter, I know your delicacy. I will remit your money to him. Where shall I tell him to return it ? "

" I will not have him return it to me. If he is rich he should be generous; there are poorer poor than I and my actors; but could I not see him? Has he forgotten his old friend, his old director? Lawrence had one of those hearts that cannot change."

" Dear Monsieur Bellamare, he would receive you only too gladly; but ought you to rekindle the fire that lurks beneath the ashes?"

" What do you mean?"

" May I ask if Mademoiselle Impéria is still a member of your society?"

" Impéria? Yes, certainly! I expect her in an hour, with the rest of my company."

" Léon, Moranbois, Anna, and Lambesq?"

" Ah well, you know us all?"

" Lawrence has told me all the chief particulars of his life. Have you still Lucinde and Régine?"

" No, they did not accompany me to America, where we have been passing the last two years, organizing, from time to time, around our little nucleus, troupes to reinforce us; but my five associates have never left me."

" And Purpurin continues in your service?"

" Always; he will die with me! Poor Purpurin!"

" What then?"

" O, we have truly had adventures; it is our fate; among others an encounter with savages converted by the missionaries and civilized, who wished to scalp us. Purpurin left them some of his hair, together with the skin. We arrived there in season

to rescue the rest. He recovered; but this little operation and the terror he experienced have not effected a perceptible improvement in his intellect. He has been forced to renounce his claims, which, after all, is not an evil. But tell, then, of Lawrence. Does he still care for Impéria?"

" More than ever."

" The deuce!"

" She never loved him?"

" Indeed, I believe she did."

" And at present."

" She denies, as always."

" Why?"

" Ah! there it is, why? I cannot tell you; perhaps dread of a life which would not suit her tastes and her theatrical habits."

" But now that he is wealthy—"

" Would he marry her now?"

" I am certain of it!"

Bellamare grew very pale, and walked in an agitated way the length of the table.

" To lose Impéria," he said, " is to lose all, for she has great ability now, and, by her friendship, her devotion, her intelligence, she is the nerve, she is the soul, of all our existences. To separate from her is to break us all up, and as for myself—"

He paused, choked by an inward sob that he repressed, walking again about the room.

" Listen to me," I said; " I am no more of the opinion that he should marry Mademoiselle de Valclos than you are. The unknown of Blois is dead, but—"

" Dead? What a pity!"

" But she has left a friend, a confidant, who loves Lawrence, who lives near him, and whom Lawrence would marry, if he could forget Impéria. I am convinced that this marriage would be much more suitable for both — "

"Tell me, then," said Bellamare, interrupting me with a preoccupied air, "how long has Madame de Valdère been dead?"

"Madame de Valdère?"

"Ah yes, her name escaped me; but what difference does that make now, since the poor unknown is no longer in the world? Her romance was so pure, she was so excellent, so virtuous, and so good a woman! You are not a man to betray that secret?"

"No, surely; but I do not understand what you say at all. Madame de Valdère is by no means dead; it is she who is the neighbor, the friend, the confidant, almost the betrothed of Lawrence."

"Ah well! — I am indeed — No, stay! Have you seen her, this neighbor?"

"Not yet. I know that she is tall, beautiful — "

"And very blond?"

"No, fair, with brown hair, according to what Lawrence has told me."

"O, hair! one has that whatever color one desires. Her first name?"

"Jeanne."

"It is she! a widow? without children? quite wealthy? twenty-eight or thirty years of age?"

"Yes, yes, yes! Lawrence has told me all that."

"Ah well, it is she; depend upon it, it is she! And Lawrence does not suspect that the friend of his un-known is his unknown herself, who represents herself as dead? That boy will always be simple and modest to the verge of blindness! O, that changes the situation indeed, my dear monsieur! Lawrence is a man of imagination. When he learns the truth, he will love again the one he loved under romantic circumstances. He will love the unknown; he will forget Impéria."

"And that will be better for him, for her, for Impéria, and for you all."

"Yes, certainly! Madame de Valdère must be warned that her feint has lasted long enough, and that she ought to reveal herself to Lawrence, because there is danger in delay, because Impéria has returned. As for me, I have not yet announced myself anywhere. The provincial journals have not printed my name. Landed at Havre two days since, I wished to gain Rouen without performing on the way. I will do still better, pass unrecognized, fire Rouen, and go to perform as far off as possible. You will not tell Lawrence of our meeting, you will not speak of me; he may think me for several months yet in Canada. Make him marry Madame de Valdère within some weeks, and all is safe."

"Then you must depart quickly; Lawrence may come to see me here, where he often comes. He may make his appearance at any moment. What would you do in that case?"

"I should tell him that Impéria had remained in America, married to a millionnaire."

"But might she not appear at the same moment? Have you not told me that you expected her?"

"Yes, we were to stop here; I had some one to see in the neighborhood, a friend who does not expect me, who will not know that I have passed. I am going to meet my troupe, so that it shall not enter this town. Adieu! Thanks! Permit me to shake your hand, and escape with all speed."

"Take back your money," I said, "since Lawrence must not know of our interview. You have time to settle this account with him."

"That is true; adieu once more."

"Do you forbid me to accompany you? I confess that I have a foolish wish to see Moranbois, Léon — "

"That is to say, Impéria. Well, come, you shall see them all, but do not mention Lawrence to them."

"That is understood."

I took my hat, and we both set out for the country. Bellamare, seeing the keeper of a livery-stable, stopped him, and bargained with him for a great omnibus, to which the horses were hastily harnessed. We sprang into it, and took the road to Caudebec.

"This omnibus," he said to me, "will receive my company and my luggage, and they will be conveyed to our destination without our having to return to the town. I will tell my companions that the friend I wished to see at Duclair no longer lives there, that the inn is bad and dear, and we will be off directly for Rouen, by way of Barentin, where we take the train."

After quarter of an hour's riding, during which time I had thoroughly enlightened Bellamare as to the state of mind in which I had left Lawrence, we hailed another omnibus, which carried the *society*. Bellamare prepared to give them the proposed explanations, and I busied myself in assisting the removal of the women and baggage, to have an opportunity of seeing all the characters of Lawrence's *roman comique*, who interested me strongly.

The first woman who sprang lightly and carelessly into the street, still covered with snow, was the little Impéria. She was very small and very thin, in fact, this woman who had played so prominent a part in my friend's life. With her close-fitting travelling-dress, her hair rolled back under her little cap of false astrakan, she looked like a little school-girl going home for the holidays, but, on observing her more attentively, I saw that she was really thirty, and that she had lost all freshness. In spite of her pure and regular features, she did not seem to me pretty. The blond, Anna, was a trifle stout to play the girlish rôles, and her cheeks, marbled by the cold, were of a very sorry color. Moranbois, entirely bald, and still wearing a cap of otter-skin, found occasion to answer me roughly when I offered to help him, in carrying a great chest, which proved that the strength of the Hercules had not diminished, in spite of time, travels, and adventures. Léon, very pale, and too closely shaved, appeared to me a man worn out and ill. He was of a distinguished type, and his extreme politeness contrasted with the rudeness of Moranbois. Lambesq was fat and ugly; he walked sideways like a crab, and complained of still feeling the rolling of the water in his legs.

Purpurin, scalped, wore a false top-piece, taken, without doubt, from the stage properties, and of a shade that did not match his hair. Truly, they were not handsome, these poor strolling actors who had seemed to me so interesting and peculiar through the narrative of Lawrence. I had leisure to examine them while Moranbois, who kept the accounts, quarrelled with the drivers, threatening them with one arm, and carrying Anna's chubby baby with the other. Impéria went up to Bellamare, who was anxious about her, and assured him, with a decided and lively air, that she was well and very happy to see the earth and trees, even leafless trees, after eighteen days on the water. She admired Normandy; she decidedly preferred the North to warm countries. In short, she talked near me for some moments, and I understood her charm and her power. When she spoke, she was transfigured; her tired, drawn features regained their elasticity. Her thinness disappeared; the transparent softness of her skin assumed a peculiar tint, half-way between marble and life. She had still magnificent teeth, and her eyes gained a penetrating brilliancy which might well become irresistible. She was one of those who do not strike, but fascinate.

Bellamare, also, looked younger to me than when I had first seen him; in a few moments, Léon produced the same impression. I attributed it to the result of a life of nervous over-excitement. Such people have no age. They always appear younger or older than they are. When I saw them depart, it seemed as if I should like to follow them to study them more closely, and then I was touched by the thought of their poverty and their honesty. They had, apparently, no means to pay for their carriage, and they returned five thousand francs to Lawrence!

I went back to the inn, where Lawrence himself awaited me. How little he suspected the thunderbolt which had just passed so near him! This morning his thoughts were taken up with Madame de Valdère. She had appeared sad and dejected since our recent interview. It was because, agitated by his confidences with me, he had allowed her to see an increase of melancholy. Now he feared lest she was secretly preparing to fly from him forever. He was angry and distressed.

"Women," said he, "have only pride; no true pity!"

He entreated me to take up my abode with him. I was engaged only for some hours in the day. He promised to carry me and bring me back every day in a conveyance swift as the wind.

"It is truly a pleasure," I said when returning with him to Berthe-ville in a carriage as elastic as a bow, drawn by three admirable horses, harnessed abreast; "it is a real pleasure thus to fly over the snow and ice, with the feet on an excellent boiler and the knees enveloped in a silky fur."

"With a friend beside one," he said, pressing my hand; "to be there alone is pleasure for a prince, and I was born a peasant. The jolts of a cart, joggled along by an old mule, are better for the health. At present, I can neither eat nor sleep. Fate is a fool who is always in error, loading those who ask nothing of her, and disappointing those who invoke her."

That evening he took me to the house of Madame de Valdère, and presented me as his only friend.

" Only ? are Bellamare, Léon, and *the others* dead ? " she asked in an agitated voice.

" It is all the same, at present," replied Lawrence. " I have not thought of them, all day, and I see no reason why the days that follow should not be like this."

Madame de Valdère turned away to serve the tea, but I saw a ray of joy upon her beautiful features. Lawrence had not exaggerated her attractions ; her beauty, her freshness, the perfection of her form, the impressive charm of her countenance, were undeniable ; her hair was naturally brown. Later, when I asked her why it had appeared blond to Lawrence and Bellamare, she told me that at that period she had had for some time a fancy for gold-powder, which was just coming in fashion. This circumstance had helped to disguise her in Lawrence's memory.

I saw in an instant that she loved him distractedly and absolutely. I desired to be alone with her, but that was impossible, without Lawrence's observing it. I resolved to write to her forthwith. While sketching in an album, I traced these words which I handed to her stealthily : " I cannot dispose of your secret without your consent. Tell the truth to Lawrence. It is necessary ! "

She went out to read it, and returned a little confused. She had not the self-possession and experience of her age ; she had still the emotion and candor of her early youth ; Lawrence was her first, her only love.

She asked him for a book that he had promised to bring her. He had forgotten it. He pretended to have left it in the pocket of his overcoat, and went out as if to bring it from the anteroom ; but he left the house, dashed out on foot through the snow and night, and ran home to get it. We heard him go out.

" We are alone," Madame de Valdère said to me ; " speak quickly."

I told her all that had transpired during the day.

" So," she said, " they are gone ? Impéria will not see him, she will not know that she is still beloved, that he is rich, that she can render him happy ! I cannot accept that. I will not owe Lawrence to a surprise, to a lie, for silence would be one. If he still loves Mademoiselle de Valclos, my fate must be fulfilled. There is still time ; he has promised me nothing ; I have made him no avowal ; I have given him no right over my life. I will depart, you shall bring Bellamare's company here ; and if this trial does not drive me from the heart of Lawrence, I will return. Tell him at once that he can rejoin them at Rouen. He will go, I am certain of it. As for me, I shall withdraw until I know my fate. Whatever it may be, I shall endure it with courage and dignity."

She burst into tears. In vain I opposed her resolution. However, I made her promise that Lawrence should know his unknown before being subjected to the decisive trial. I persuaded her to go and put on gold-dust and a black mantle, that she might appear as he had seen her in the blue room.

When she returned, blond and veiled, I made her turn her back to the door where Lawrence would re-enter and I withdrew. I met him all out of breath, bringing the vol-ume. I told him that I was seized with a violent headache, and that his neighbor had permitted me to retire.

He returned very late; I had gone to bed. He came to throw himself upon my neck; he was intoxicated with love and happiness. Bellamare had not been deceived. The man of imagination had resumed his nor-mal existence. He adored two wo-men in Madame de Valdère,—the unknown, who had haunted his dreams; the friend, who had gener-ously labored to effect his cure. He wished to marry her the next day. He would have done so had the thing been possible.

Had she informed him of Impé-ria's return? He said not a word about it to me, and I dared not question him. I confess that, on see-ing Lawrence's intoxication, and hear-ing him make the plans of a million-naire lover who wishes to lavish all upon his idol, I thought, with a cer-tain oppression at the heart, of the poor little actress who went away without gloves, and almost without cloak, over the snowy road in pur-suit of a cruel profession, with her talent, her nerve, her will, her forced smiles and tears, for all capital, for

all future. Hitherto I had pitilessly worked in behalf of her rival. I sur-prised myself thinking the latter too easily happy. Left alone, I could not sleep again. Some anxiety preyed upon me, and I asked my-self if I had been right in acting as I had done.

I dressed myself, and, as I contem-plated a fine winter sunrise from my window, I saw in the court-yard a man wrapped in a goat-skin coat, and wearing a woollen cap, who re-sembled a bargeman of the Seine, and who was making signs to me. I went down, and, approaching him, I recognized Bellamare.

"Show me," he said "to the house of Madame de Valdère. I must speak to her unknown to Lawrence. I know that he went to bed late; we shall have time. I will tell you on the way what brings me."

I pointed out the path; I ran to put on another coat and rejoined him.

"You see," said he, "I have re-traced my steps. At Barentin I embarked all my company for Rou-en. I journeyed all night in a wretched stage-wagon; but I was tormented, I was feverish, I did not feel the cold. I had resolved to per-form a bad act, a cowardice, through selfishness! I cannot carry it out. It would be the first of my life. Impéria has always sacrificed her-self for her friends. She might have been engaged at Paris, had a great success there, and made a fortune, or at least have found an easy and com-fortable existence there. There is more than one belonging to the Thé-âtre Français who does not equal her.

She refused, in order not to leave us. You know how she acted, when she was overwhelmed with the gifts of Prince Klémenti and his guests. You have divined that in refusing Lawrence's love, it was still that she wished to devote herself to us. That cannot last forever. She is thirty now. She is weak, exhausted. Our little company will never make a fortune; our life will be a perpetual drag. Some years more still laughing and singing, she will succumb to illness; that is how we finish!—and here she can have a hundred thousand francs a year, and an excellent, charming husband, who still loves her, who will be happy in making her happy. And I should conceal it from her! No, I ought not, I will not. I will see Madame de Valdère, for I swore to her formerly to serve her cause. She must know that I abandon it, that I ought to abandon it. She is a woman of very large heart, I know. I met her more than once after the adventure of Blois, and I had always that I could give her hope. All is changed since the time when Impéria rejected Lawrence with a grief that it was impossible to hide from me. At that time we were leaving for America. I did not see the Countess then. She was travelling. I did not know where to write her. She must know all, and, in her supreme delicacy, she must pronounce. As for me, there is one thing certain, I cannot deceive Impéria, and I will not. After that let these two women dispute the heart of my former young *premier*, or let the more generous yield him to the other; it is no longer

my affair. I shall have done my duty."

I was too much of Bellamare's opinion to contradict him. We had Madame de Valdère awakened. She listened to us weeping, and remained powerless, speechless, irresolute, defenceless. She was weak but admirable, for she uttered not a word of complaint. She thought only of Lawrence's happiness, and concluded thus: "I know that he loves me, I am sure of it now. He told me so yesterday, with a passion so convincing that I should not respect him if I doubted it; but he has been sick in mind and heart so long a time, that I shall not be surprised to see him escape me again. I have no right to rebel against this decree of fate. I accepted him in advance, when I came to establish myself near him, with the intention of making him love me for myself, without fiction or poetry. In passing myself off as a friend of the unknown, my object was to know and understand thoroughly the feeling he had had for her. I saw that this love was nothing more than a transient emotion, a chapter in the wandering romance of his life, although he spoke of her with respect and gratitude. I feared then to appear too romantic myself to him by revealing my secret, and, in order to give him that confidence in me which he had lacked in her, I showed him that I knew how to be an unselfish, generous, and tender friend. He realized it; but this friendship was still too new to banish the memory of Impéria. I felt it; I saw it. I wished to wait still, to preserve myself free toward him, to render my affection necessary to him, and to confess the past to him only on giving him the future. I was forced yesterday to betray myself. He was excited, intoxicated; and I, I was cowardly, I could not resolve to tell him that Impéria was so near him. You come this morning to tell me that I must complete the trial. Ah well, you crush me. I was so happy in seeing him happy at my feet! No matter, you are right. I will do what you wish."

And again she wept openly, and as if from a full heart. She made Bellamare weep.

"Come, my dear madame," I said to her, "I am not very impressible, and not at all romantic, and yet I feel that you are an angel, the good angel of Lawrence probably; but, in your interest, ought we to expose you to some reproach in the future, if he discovers the truth in three respects, which are, that Impéria has returned, that she is free, and that she perhaps loves him? Do you not fear that in a day of nervous discomfort, a rainy day in the country, one of those days when one would commit a crime without a reason, he may complain of us all for our silence, and of you in particular?"

"It is not a question of myself," she said; "do not think of me! I have a faithful and reflective, not an exuberant, nature. I waited for a long time, and for a long time I lived in a dream that faded and revived alternately; I travelled; I improved myself; I grew calm; I even formed other plans; and if I could love no other man than Lawrence, it was against my will. I desired to forget him. Whatever happens to me, I will not kill myself, and I will keep myself from violent despair. I shall still have had three months of happiness in my life, and the few hours of pure and perfect joy last night. What it concerns us to know, what I absolutely will know, is which of us, Impéria or I, will give most happiness to Lawrence."

"And how shall we know it?" said Bellamare, who was plunged again into his perplexity. "Who can read the future? The one who will make him the happiest will be the one who will love him most."

"No," replied Madame de Valdère, "for she who will love him best will be the one who will sacrifice herself. Listen, we must be extricated from this dilemma; I will see Impéria; she shall explain herself. I have a right to preserve Lawrence from a new grief, if she loves him but little or not at all."

"How will you arrange all that without his knowledge?" said Bellamare. "Is he not with you every day?"

"I have, at this moment, complete dominion over him. He entreated me yesterday to fix the day of our marriage. I will send him to Paris for my papers. I will warn my notary, by a telegraphic despatch, to make him wait for them several days. Go and bring Impéria from Rouen, and give me your word that you will tell her nothing yet. It is from me, from me alone, that she should learn the truth."

Bellamare gave his word, and departed on the instant. I went to arouse Lawrence, who hastened directly to the house of her whom he already called his betrothed and with whom he was already madly in love. She had the courage to conceal her agitation and her terror from him, and seem to yield to his impatience. That evening he departed for Paris.

In the night the train which took him to Rouen must have met that which brought Bellamare and Impéria to Barentin.

The latter arrived on the following morning. I awaited them at Madame de Valdère's, ready to withdraw when they approached.

"No," she said to me; "Impéria does not know you, and would be embarrassed to explain herself before you; but I am extremely anxious that you should give an account, a minute and faithful account, of this interview to Lawrence. Pass into my boudoir, from which you can hear everything. Listen to us; take notes, if necessary. I insist upon it."

I obeyed. Impéria entered alone. Bellamare, not wishing to impede the confidences of the two women, ascended to an apartment that had been prepared for him. Madame de Valdère received Impéria, extending both hands to her and embracing her.

"M. Bellamare," she said, "must have forewarned you somewhat?"

"He told me," responded Impéria in her clear and steady voice, "that a charming, good, beautiful, and accomplished lady had seen me formerly upon the stage, — I know not where! —and had deigned to take a liking to me; that this lady, knowing that I was in the vicinity, desired to make an important communication to me. I placed reliance on it, and I came."

"Yes," replied Madame de Valdère, "you were right. I have a great esteem for you; but you are tired, it is perhaps too soon — "

"No, madame, I am never tired."

"You are cold."

"I am inured to all."

"Take a cup of chocolate that I have had prepared for you."

"I see tea also. I should prefer it."

"I will serve you; pray, pray permit me. Poor child! how hard is this life you lead for so delicate a person!"

"I have never complained of it."

"Still, you were reared in comfort, in luxury even. I know your birth."

"As you are kind we will not talk of that; I never speak of it myself."

"I know it; but I have a right to put one question to you. If you should be wealthy again, would you not gladly leave the stage?"

"No, madame, never."

"It is a passion then?"

"Yes, a passion."

"Exclusive of any other?"

Impéria kept silence.

"Pardon me," continued Madame de Valdère, in a still more agitated voice, "I am indiscreet; I am doomed to be so. My duty is to question you, to obtain your confidence without reserve. If you refuse me — But do you not see that you would be wrong, that I am a sincere person? Stay! do not think my object is to convert you; it concerns a very different matter! I am the devoted friend of a man who loved you deeply, and who, now very rich and free from every tie, could love you again."

"You speak of Lawrence, madame; I learned yesterday, from the conversation of people in the carriage with me, that the former actor had inherited a great fortune."

"Ah well?"

"Ah well, what? I rejoiced for him."

"And for yourself?"

"For myself? is that what you wish to know? Well, no, madame, I did not think of myself."

"You never loved him then?" cried Madame de Valdère, who could not conceal her joy.

"I loved him tenderly, and his memory will always be dear to me," replied Impéria, firmly; "but I did not wish to become his wife."

"Why? Have you retained the prejudices of rank?"

"I never had them."

"Are you really engaged?"

"In my own eyes, yes."

"You are so still?"

"Always."

The Countess could no longer contain herself; she clasped Mademoiselle de Valclos in her arms.

"I see madame," said the latter, "that you take an interest in me of which I am not the principal object. Permit me to reassure you entirely, and to tell you that really and truly another affection separates me forever from Lawrence."

"Ah well, save him, save me, wholly. See him and tell him so."

"Why should I? I told him so seriously when we met at Clermont for the last time?"

"But you wept then; he thought that you loved him."

"He told you that?"

"It was M. Bellamare who told me."

"Ah yes; Bellamare thinks, also, that I loved him!"

"And that you love him still."

"He will soon be undeceived; but tell me, madame, if my reply had been opposite to what it has been, what would you have done?"

"My dear child, I had taken a great resolution, and I should have kept it. I should have gone away, without reproach, without weakness, and without resentment against you."

"You are the unknown of Blois!"

"Bellamare has told you?"

"No, I guess it."

"It is I, in fact; by what do you recognize me?"

"By your generosity! This is not the first time that you have been ready to act thus. Did you not write to Bellamare? Did you not charge him to speak to me from you?"

"Yes. He did so?"

"He did it without telling me your name, which I have only learned to-day. In the carriage where I heard of Lawrence's brilliant position, some one said, 'He will marry his neighbor, Madame de Valdère.' So be happy without scruple and without alarm, dear madame. I heard it with great pleasure. I love Lawrence like a brother."

"Swear it, dear child, it was as a brother that you wept for him."

"I see that my tears will remain upon your mind; my confidence must respond to your own. You shall know all in few words, for you are familiar with my whole life, except the secret history of my feelings."

"Tell me, tell me all!" cried Madame de Valdère.

Impéria reflected for a moment, and thus related her history.

"You know how and why I entered the theatre. Lawrence must have told you. I wished to support my father, and, in spite of all the changes of my life, I succeeded in giving him, until his last day, as much comfort as he could appreciate in the state of mild insanity to which he was reduced. I went to see him every year; he did not recognize me; but I assured myself that he lacked for nothing, and became tranquil again. It was M. Bellamare who enabled me to perform this duty, and it is of M. Bellamare that I am going to speak to you. When, for the first time, I went to him secretly to ask him to make me an actress, he was not a stranger to me. He had come to organize and direct a play to be performed by children and intimate friends that we were preparing at Valclos for my poor father's birthday. I was twelve years old. Bellamare was still young. His pleasant ugliness diverted me at first; then his wit, his kindness, his tender grace with the children, captivated my childish heart and took possession of it forever."

"What!" cried Madame de Valdère, "it is Bellamare whom you love? Is it possible?"

"It is he," answered Mademoiselle de Valclos, firmly; "it is this poor man who has always been ugly, who will soon be old, and who will always remain poor. Look at me; I shall soon be like him; time has well

effaced the differences! When I was twelve he was thirty, and my eyes did not reckon. When he made me rehearse my part and study my gestures, and when he paternally encouraged me, by telling me that I was a born artist, I was filled with a great pride, and the memory of the man who had uttered the sentence of my destiny impressed itself upon my mind like the touch of a mysterious spirit come from another sphere to warn me of my vocation. The day when he left Valclos the little boys whom he had taught to act in our performance threw themselves upon his neck. He was so kind, so gay, he governed them so well while he amused them, that all adored them. He came to me and said, 'Mademoiselle Jane, do not be afraid! I shall not ask permission to kiss you. I am too ugly and you are too pretty. But my hand is not so ugly as my face; will you put your little hand into it?'

"I was touched; his hand was very beautiful. I forgot his face, I threw my arms about his neck and kissed him on both cheeks. His face felt soft and smooth; he was always very careful of his person. From that moment he never seemed ugly to me.

"When he had gone they talked of him considerably at our house. My father, who was an accomplished and very literary man, had the highest opinion of Bellamare's intellect and character. He treated him as a man of culture, and considered him a genuine artist. Bellamare had great success in our province, where he was then playing. My parents

often attended these performances.
I persuaded them one day to let me
accompany them. He acted Figaro.
He wore a rich costume in the part,
was full of vivacity, elegance, and
grace ; he appeared charming to me.
His very defects, his bad voice,
pleased me. It was impossible to
separate his physical disadvantages
from his good qualities. They applauded him passionately. I was
exalted by his success. They permitted me to throw him a bouquet,
whose ribbon bore these words, ' Little Jane to her professor.' He raised
the bouquet to his lips, looking at
me tenderly. I was intoxicated with
pride. My little cousins shared my
excitement; they knew the celebrated
actor, the applauded, triumphant artist! They had performed with him ;
they had called him ' thou,' he had
addressed them gravely as ' My dear
comrades.' They could not be prevented from going to embrace him in
the greenroom, between the acts. He
handed them a photograph for me
which represented him in his pretty
costume of Figaro, and he said to
them, ' You will tell your cousin to
look at this phiz, when she has some
little trouble ; it will make her wish
to laugh again.'

" He was far from grotesque in
this rôle, and the photograph had
chanced to flatter him. I received
it with pride ; I guarded it with a
religious care ; not only did I cease
to think him ugly, but I thought
him handsome.

" Love is more precocious with
young girls than is supposed ; I was
still a child ; I felt no agitation of
the senses, but my imagination was

invaded by a type, and my heart
swayed by a preference. I made no
mystery of it; I was too innocent for
that. They felt no anxiety about it;
they attached no importance to it;
and as they spoke of Bellamare only
to praise his honor, his talent, his
literary attainments, his good breeding, and the charm of his conversation, nothing combated my ideal.

" When the age of reason came, I
talked no longer of him, but I
dreamed of being an actress and did
not plume myself upon it. Every
year we acted a new play to celebrate
my father's birthday. Bellamare
was no longer there, but I strove to
act better and better. They considered me remarkable ; I believed myself to be so ; I rejoiced at it. I
cared only for dramatic literature.
I learned and knew by heart all
the classic repertory. I even wrote
very silly little plays, and I composed grand verses, very awkward,
doubtless, but which my kind
father thought admirable. He encouraged my taste and suspected
nothing.

" You know under what mournful
circumstances I sought Bellamare, to
confide my misfortunes and my
schemes to him. In this secret interview I saw that he was profoundly agitated; at first sight he had appeared to me much older. His softened and brilliant glance rejuvenated
him at once in my eyes. It was
there that I first became conscious of
the sentiment with which he inspired
me, and I had a thrill of terror when
I thought that he might read my
feelings.

" He would have loved me, loved

me passionately, I know, now that I have seen him love other women; but his love was a flash that disappeared as suddenly as it came. Bellamare is the true artist of another time, with all the ardent qualities, all the frank eccentricities, all the impulses, all the weariness, that result from a life of carelessness and over-excitement. He would have loved me and forsaken me, aided and assisted me, but forgotten me like the others. Had I fixed his affections, he could not have married me; he was married already.

"I did not divine all this at our first meeting; but I distrusted myself, and, recovering my self-possession, I showed such firmness and seriousness, that he speedily changed in face and accent. He swore to be my father; he has kept his word.

"And as for me, I have always loved him, although he has caused me much suffering, by leading the life of a man of pleasure before my eyes; never speaking of his adventures, — he has too much reserve and modesty, — but not always able to conceal his emotions. There were quite long intervals, when I believed that I loved him no longer, and congratulated myself on never having confided my secret to any one. My pride, too often wounded, is the very simple cause of my invincible discretion. If I had confessed the truth to Lawrence, or to any other, I should have seen them laugh bitterly at my folly. I could not resolve to be ridiculous. My silence and the persistency of my affection have prevented me from being so. Bellamare, not suspecting the nature of my attachment,

has never entertained wrong feelings toward me.

"One sole disturbance was produced in the equilibrium that I maintained. The love of Lawrence troubled me and made me suffer. I have promised to tell you all; I will conceal nothing from you.

"The first time that I noticed him he did not please me. When, from childhood, one's favorite type has been a smiling and tender face, handsome features with a gloomy look, that somewhat menacing expression imparted by a love that is forcibly restrained, cause more alarm than sympathy. I was very sincere when I told Lawrence that I did not like handsome men. I was touched by his devotion, I appreciated his noble character; but, when you saw him at Blois, I felt absolutely nothing more for him than for Léon, although his society was more agreeable and better suited me. When he left us, it did not trouble me much. When I found him again seriously ill at Paris, I nursed him as I should have nursed Léon or Moranbois. The poor care for each other, without any of that prudent reserve that the rich can maintain toward each other even to their death-bed. We cannot easily procure a substitute; we assist each other personally; perhaps we love each other more.

"You must know, besides, from Lawrence, what sort of friendship, cordial, familiar, confidential, their intimate mode of life creates among members of a theatre. They quarrel frequently; but each reconciliation strengthens the fraternal bond; they are offended at a trifle; they carry their penitence to excess. Our company experienced great reverses; you know our shipwreck, the tragic death of Marco, our adventures with brigands, our misfortunes, our dangers, our sufferings, all the cases of excitement which made this general friendship a sort of collective intoxication. It was at this period, on our return from this affecting campaign, that the love of Lawrence began to trouble me. I saw clearly that he had not conquered it and that he was suffering from it still. When he returned to declare it to me openly, I had that time suffered in his absence on my own account.

"Bellamare had vexed me greatly, without knowing it. He had learned of the death of his wife. He had spoken of marrying again, in order to have a friend, a companion, a perpetual associate; and he had frankly consulted me, telling me that he had thought of Anna. She was rather young for him, he said; but she had had several lovers and two children. She must long for a tranquil life, for, by nature, she was sensible. With a good husband she would be so cheerfully and without regret.

"I showed no pique. I spoke to Anna, who laughed at the idea; she adored Bellamare, but like a daughter. It was a woman of Régine's age and style, she said, who would suit our beloved director.

"I was crestfallen; but when I wished to return this answer to Bellamare, he hardly knew what I was talking about. He had forgotten his fancy. He laughed at marriage; he declared himself incapable of having a faithful wife, because it would be necessary to practise what one preached. He said that when he spoke of Anna to me, the evening before, he was completely carried away by the rôle of husband he had just been playing in Emile Augier's *Gabrielle*. He had longed for a family; he adored children. He had never had any. That was why he thought of marriage 'at least once every ten years!'

"I felt very foolish and very much humiliated. I swore to myself that he should never suspect my love. Lawrence arrived, in the mean time, and his passion bewildered me. I felt that I was a woman, that I was forever alone in life, that happiness was in my reach, perhaps, that my refusal was unjust and cruel; that I was going to break the most generous, most faithful and purest heart. I came near saying, 'Yes, let us depart together!'

"But that lasted only a moment; for while Lawrence was speaking to me I saw Bellamare sauntering at a distance, in a dejected attitude, and I remembered that, in giving myself up to another love, I should have to forswear, to bury forever, that which had filled my life with courage, honor, and labor. This man, whom I had loved since my childhood, who had loved me so reverently in spite of the lightness of his habits, who venerated me as a divinity, and who did not love me because he loved me too much, it would be necessary never too see him again. That immense respect he had for me he would not have for another. That unvarying devotion I had had for him, in what woman's heart would he find it again? When one spoke to another of loving Bellamare, she laughed! I, alone, was obstinate enough to wish to be the companion of his poverty, the support of his old age, the rehabilitation of his ugliness. I alone, who had never inspired him with desire, knew the pure, religious, and truly great side of this variable soul, ardently in love with the ideal. I saw the lines come on his forehead, his eyes grow hollow, and his laugh less free; and there were moments of profound weariness which made his acting more confused, his attacks of sensibility more nervous, sometimes whimsical. Bellamare felt the first approach of discouragement, for he urged me to marry Lawrence, and I perceived in him a sort of despair, like that of a father who casts his only daughter into the arms of a husband who will take her away forever.

"I saw the future, the troupe soon separated, the association broken up, Bellamare, alone, seeking new companions, falling into the hands of adventurers and knaves. I knew well that my influence over him and the others, the support that I had always given to Moranbois's rigid economy, the gentleness that I had used to soothe the secret and ever-increasing bitterness of Léon, my remonstrances with Anna to prevent her from flying away with the first new-comer, had alone secured, for a long time past, this continually floating chain, whose links I always fastened patiently again. And I was going to leave this excellent man, this noble artist, this tender father, this friend of fifty, because he lacked the youth and beauty of Lawrence!

"I was horrified at this idea; I wept foolishly, without being able to conceal it from the one whom my selfishness regretted and whom my firmness crushed; but while weeping before him, while sobbing on the breast of Bellamare, who comprehended nothing of it, I renewed to God my vow never to abandon him, and I consoled myself for Lawrence's departure, because I was satisfied with my conduct.

"And now that three years have elapsed since my sacrifice, three years which must certainly have cured Lawrence, and during which I have been more than ever necessary and useful to Bellamare, for I have seen him, mature at last, take heed of the morrow, from affection for me, deprive himself of useless pleasures to devote himself to me when I was ill, renounce dissipations which had hitherto had dominion over him, in the fear of wasting the personal resources which he wished to consecrate to me; in a word, act like a man of prudence and self-control, the most impossible thing for him, in the sole design of sustaining me, in case of need: it is now that I should regret not being rich by the provision of another? I should confess to Lawrence that I could have loved him, I should return to him, because he has inherited his uncle's fortune? And you would esteem me? and he could esteem me still? and I should not be ashamed of myself? No, madame, fear nothing; I have studied *Chimène* in the text too much not to have understood and adopted the Spanish device, *Soy quien soy.* I remember too well that my father was a man of honor, to lack dignity. I have loved Bellamare too much to lose the habit of preferring him to all. You may say to Lawrence all that I have just said to you; you may even add that at present I am sure of Bellamare, and that at an early day I intend to offer him my hand. And if it is true, if it is possible, that Lawrence still has some emotion in recalling the past, be sure that he loves Bellamare too much to be jealous of the one who was his best friend. Now, embrace me, without fear or effort, and consider that you have in me a heart most devoted to your cause, most disinterested for your happiness."

"Ah! my dear Impéria," cried the Countess, who clasped her in her arms, "what a woman you are! In my days of pride, I often figured in my own eyes as a grand heroine of romance! How far below you I have always been, I who based my glory on knowing how to wait far off and without danger, while you devoted yourself to the martyrdom of waiting, with the spectacle of so many disenchantments before your eyes! When I waited thus, I knew that Lawrence, secluded in his village, and sacrificing all to filial duty, purified himself, and unconsciously rendered himself worthy of me. And you, following the footsteps of the one you loved, you perceived his faults, you shared his misfortunes, and you were not discouraged!"

"Let us talk no more of myself," said Impéria; "let us think of what you must do that we may all be happy."

"I will speak to Bellamare," replied Madame de Valdère, quickly.

It was unnecessary, Bellamare had rejoined me in the boudoir. He had heard all he was almost suffocated by surprise; then, seized suddenly with a great excitement, he rushed into the drawing-room, and, addressing Madame de Valdère and Impéria, he cried,—

"O excellent women! how cruel you are, without knowing it! What faults, what stains you would spare us, if you would take us for what we are, in love, children ready to receive the impulse that you give them!— Impéria! Impéria! if I had suspected sooner! See what comes from guarding myself from presumption! See what it is to be neither assuming, nor selfish, nor calculating in anything! How you have punished me for it, you, who with a word could have rendered me worthy of you ten years earlier! And here I am old, and now perhaps unworthy of the happiness that you will give me! No, I do not believe it, notwithstanding, and I would not have you believe it. I am willing that all should be as it is! Ah, this dream that I have never dared to tell, I have had it a thousand times, and you have not suspected it! I have loved you madly, Impéria, loved you wrongly, I acknowledge, since I thought only of forgetting it, or defending myself from it by every means. I wished to marry you to Lawrence; I wished to divert my thoughts by intoxicating, transient pleasures. You suffered from them, when you could so easily have restrained me! What is woman's pride, then? A great and fine thing, I admit, but a torture of which we know only the severity, and do not see the use! Confess that you have doubted me too much; confess it, if you do not wish me to despise myself for having doubted too much also!—And you, madame," he said, turning to the Countess, "you have acted like her; it is the romance of a generous woman then! Ah well, it is not generous at all, since it delays happiness for the sake of some ideal that you seek, until the meridian of life, when it is within your reach—"

"You rebuke us," said Impéria; "would not one say that we were the guilty ones, and you—"

"Hush! hush!" exclaimed Bellamare, still more carried away; "you do not see that I am mad with pride just now, that I justify myself, that I defend myself, and—a thing that never happened to me before—that I love and admire myself? Since you love me, I must be something great and excellent. Let me imagine it, for, if I should return to my former opinion of myself, I should fear for your reason. Let me ramble on, let me be insane, or I must explode!"

He went on talking, somewhat at random, like an actor who, not finding his rôle exalted to the pitch of his emotion, improvises unconsciously. It was easy to see that he had loved Impéria more ardently than she had wished to believe, and that the fear of ridicule, so powerful with a mind accustomed to represent the absurd in human nature, had paralyzed his impulses on all occasions. He ended by weeping like a child;

and, as I desired to speak of Lawrence and arrange something with Madame de Valdère, he confessed that he had lost his head, and could think only of himself. He rushed out into the wood, where we saw him running and talking to himself like one insane. I wondered at this power of personal emotion, whose fire, so often kindled for the benefit of others, burned still in him as in a young man.

Five days later Lawrence returned to Bertheville; he found Madame de Valdère there, who was waiting for him in order to give him a great surprise. He brought back all the documents necessary for the approaching publication of their banns. She did not allow him to talk of their affairs and plans; this evening must be devoted to the happiness of meeting again, and recalling the past in sweet tranquillity.

I arrived, as she had bidden me, when dinner was over. Not only had I been initiated into what was going to happen, but I had taken an active part in it, and I must not lose sight of Lawrence while the Countess was away from him. She had left us to make an exquisite toilet, which she completed very quickly; and when she returned for Lawrence to conduct her to the drawing-room, she was dazzling. It was certainly enough to turn his head, and cause him to forget the interesting but wasted Impéria. In the saloon she said to him, "I have played the mistress here in your absence, as if I were already at home. You are to take coffee in the great hall below, whose complete restoration I have hastened, for I was anxious to let you see this beautiful work ended, the wainscots finished, the inlaid floor polished, the old lustres hung and lighted. They have also tried the fire there, which is charming. Nothing smokes; come and see, and if you are not satisfied with my management, do not tell me so; I should feel too badly."

We passed into the great apartment whose use had not yet been decided by Lawrence. It was an old council-chamber, fully equal to that of Saint Vandrille. The architecture was so well preserved, and the wainscots of so good a style, that he had desired and effected its restoration without other object than the love of repairing. He admired the general effect, and did not ask why a large green curtain cut off and concealed all the farther part. He thought that this hid the scaffolding that they had not had time to remove. The secret of our rapid preparations had not transpired. He really suspected nothing. Then a little invisible orchestra, that we had procured from Rouen, played a classic overture; the coarse canvas which concealed the back fell and disclosed another curtain of red and gold, that revealed the front of a pretty little improvised stage.

Lawrence started.

"What is it?" he said; "a play? I care for them no longer; I could not listen to it."

"It will be short," replied the Countess. "Your workmen, whose affections you have gained, have planned to give you this diversion; it will be very simple; meet it in the same spirit, and think kindly of the intention."

"Bah!" said Lawrence; "they will be pretentious and ridiculous!"

He looked at the programme; it was a performance made up of fragments. They were going to play the night-scenes three, eight, and nine of the fifth act of the "Marriage of Figaro."

"Come!" said Lawrence, "they are mad, these good people; but I have been so bad an Almaviva in my time, that I have a right to hiss no one."

The curtain rose. Figaro was on the stage. It was Bellamare in a handsome costume, walking about, in the obscurity of the scene, with inimitable grace and naturalness. I know not if Lawrence recognized him at once. As for me I hardly knew him. I was unused to these sudden transformations. I thought the whole secret lay in the costume and the paint. I did not know that the actor of ability really grows younger by some mysterious operation of his inward feeling. Bellamare was admirably formed and still supple. He had a fine elastic leg, a slender waist, graceful shoulders, head well proportioned and well set on. His rose-colored net harmonized skilfully its vivid hue with the sorber paint on his cheeks. His small black eyes were fine diamonds. His teeth, still handsome, flashed in the half-light of the simulated night upon the stage. He looked thirty at most; he seemed charming to me. I dreaded to hear his defective voice. He spoke the opening words of the scene, *O femme! femme! femme!*

créature décevante! and this peculiar voice, affected by some very perceptible inward sadness, did not
shock me more than that of Samson,
which had so often moved and penetrated me. He continued. He
spoke so well! This monologue is
so charming, and he had so finely
studied and understood it! I cannot say if I was influenced by all I
knew of his real character, but the
actor appeared admirable to me. I
forgot his age ; I understood the obstinate love of Impéria; I applauded
him with enthusiasm.

Lawrence was mute and motionless. His eyes were fixed ; he
seemed changed into a statue. He
held his breath ; he did not seek to
comprehend what he saw. The
sweat stood in drops upon his forehead, when passing to scene eight,
Suzanne entered and began the dia-
logue with Figaro. It was Impéria!
Madame de Valdère was pale as
death. Lawrence, divining her anxiety, turned to her, took her hand
and held it to his lips all the time
that the scene lasted. It is a rapid
love-duet in warm colors. The two
friends played it with fervor. Impéria appeared as much younger as
Bellamare ; she was full of fire and
animation ; one would have said that
the poor weary actress had vitality
enough and to spare.

Lambesq came next, to represent
with more energy than discrimina-
tion the anger of Almaviva. Chérubin showed himself a moment, with
the features of Anna, whose precocious *embonpoint* seemed to have
vanished, she wore her page's dress
so easily and prettily. Moranbois

appeared, also, beneath the great hat
of Basile, which lent additional hol-
lowness to his pale and withered face.
They said only a few words. Léon
had outlined a rapid closing scene
which would serve as *dénouement*,
and remove the necessity of such
parts as were lacking. They had
only wished to show themselves to
Lawrence, alive and well, and make
last year's roses bloom for him a
moment amid the snows of winter.
Léon expressed to him, in the name
of all, this tender and fraternal sentiment in a few well-turned and well-
spoken verses.

Lawrence then rushed toward them
with open arms, at the same time
that they sprang lightly from the
platform to hasten to him. Madame
de Valdère breathed again, on seeing
that her betrothed embraced Impéria
like the others, with as much joy and
as little embarrassment.

Lawrence, on seeing the noble girl
also embrace Madame de Valdère
with effusion, understood what had
passed between them.

"We have all learned your happiness," said Impéria to him ; "we
wished to tell you ours. Bellamare
and I, betrothed a long time since,
decided in America to be married on
our return to France. So our visit
is to impart that information to
you."

Lawrence uttered an exclamation
of surprise.

"And yet," said he, " I had thought
of it twenty times!"

"And you could not believe it?"
said Bellamare. " I, who had never
thought of it in all that time, cannot
believe it yet. It is so improbable !

Are you jealous of my prospects?" he added, in an undertone.

"No," answered Lawrence in the same key, "you deserve her, exactly because you did not seek her. If I were still in love with her, your happiness would console me for my wound; but the unknown triumphed when she revealed herself; I am hers, and truly hers, forever!"

The actors went to take off their costumes. Lawrence, at the feet of the Countess, — in the saloon which I nearly entered thoughtlessly, and from which I withdrew before they had perceived me, — blessed her delicate confidence, and swore that she should never repent it.

I strolled off, a little curiously, after the actors. I met Impéria, who had changed her costume, and reappeared in a very handsome toilet which still looked fresh, although she had worn it a number of times, she told me, in playing *La Dame aux Camellias* at New York. In another room I perceived Moranbois, and thought I could enter, but drew back, somewhat surprised, on seeing Chérubin there with her baby. The child was laughing as he drew his fat rosy fingers over the gilt buttons of the page's vest.

"Enter, enter," cried the travestied actress; "come and see how beautiful he is!"

She lifted him up, and raising him in her arms she pressed the infant to her breast, purified by this passionate embrace.

"This dear love," she added, "will never know another parent than his mother, and he will be very fortunate! He will have only me! His father, who does not care for him, is an angel to me, since he leaves him to my sole possession."

"You do not fear," said I, as I admired the boy, who was magnificent, "that this life may agitate and fatigue him?"

"No, no," she answered. "I have lost two that they induced me to put out to nurse, on the pretext that they would be better cared for. I resolved that, if I had the happiness to have another, it should not leave me. Can a child be ill in the arms of his mother? This one is always in the greenroom when I play, and he does not cry; he knows already that he must not cry there. He is pleased to see me in my costume; he loves tinsel. He is wild with joy when I am rouged; he adores feathers!"

"And he will be an actor?" I inquired.

"Certainly, so as not to leave me; besides, if it is the hardest of professions, it is still the one in which, from time to time, one finds most happiness."

"Come!" said Moranbois, "dress yourself, and give me my godson."

He took the child, addressed him tenderly as *Toad*, and carried him up and down the corridors, singing to him in his cavernous falsetto voice, some air impossible to recognize, but which the little fellow relished greatly, and attempted to sing also, after his fashion.

An exquisite and charming supper reassembled us all from midnight until six o'clock in the morning. The Venetian glasses flashed their vivid colors in the light of the waxtapers. Hothouse flowers, raised at various heights upon a circular stage, surrounded us with spring-like perfumes, while the snow continued to heap the park, lighted by the full moon. We were noisier, we eight, than a band of students. We talked all together, we touched glasses at every recollection, and then we amused ourselves by hearing Bellamare describe, with an incomparable charm that Lawrence had not in the least exaggerated, his campaign in America; a musical rehearsal, in which they had sworn to continue without interruption and to keep time, while passing the rapids of the St. Lawrence in a steamer; a night of merry-making at Quebec, when they had supped by the light of the *aurora borealis*; a night of distress when they were lost in the virgin forest; days of fatigue and fasting in the desert beyond the great lakes; an unpleasant encounter with savages, another with troops of bisons; great ovations in California, where they had had Chinese for machinists, etc. When he had captivated us by these recitals, he made us laugh and sing; then we paused, to listen to the great winter silence outside; and these moments of reflection penetrated Lawrence with a feeling of moral, intellectual, and physical repose, whose solemn sweetness he at last appreciated.

Madame de Valdère was adorable. She amused herself like a child; she called Impéria "thou," and the latter returned it, in order not to wound her. Occasionally she addressed Bellamare in the same way, without perceiving it. Bellamare was already her old friend and tried con-

fidant. Between her and Impéria, those two irreproachable women, to whom he had been a father, he felt absolved, he said, from his former sins.

Purpurin served us, travestied as a negro.

When the supper was ended, Lawrence addressed Moranbois, giving him his ancient *sobriquet*, which the Hercules permitted only to his best friends.

"Coq-en-bois," he said, "where is your cash-box? I am still a member of the association; I wish to see the bottom of your cash-box."

"That is easy," replied the steward, coolly. "We came here for the precise purpose of settling our account with you."

And he drew from his pocket a massive pocket-book, worn and locked, from which he took five bank-notes.

"We know your trick!" replied Lawrence; "pass me your utensil."

He looked at the pocket-book; the sum which they returned him deducted, there remained three hundred francs.

"Eternal *boulotteurs*!" said Lawrence, laughing, "it is very fortunate that you have played properly this evening! Come, my wife," he said, addressing the Countess, "since this evening we 'thou' each other, bring the receipts of our artists; it is for you to estimate them."

She kissed him on the forehead, before us all, took the key which he held out to her, disappeared, and returned quickly.

When she had filled and stuffed the steward's pocket-book, there were bills to the amount of two hundred thousand francs in the cash-box.

"Do not say a word," she said to Bellamare; "half of it is mine; it is Impéria's dowry."

"I made over, to-day, my part of the profits to my godson," said Moranbois, with undisturbed composure.

"And I mine to Bellamare," said Léon. "I have also inherited from an uncle, not a millionnaire, but I have enough to live on."

"And you leave us?" said Bellamare, dropping the pocket-book in dismay. "O fortune! if you separate us, you are good for nothing but to stir our punch!"

"I, I leave you!" exclaimed Léon, also pale, but with the inspired air of an author who has thought of his *dénouement*, "never! for me it is too late! Inspiration is a mad thing which desires an impossible situation. If I become a true poet, it will be on condition of not becoming a man of sense. And then—" added he, with a little confusion, "Anna, it seems to me that I hear your child crying."

She rose, and passed into the next room, where the infant slumbered in his cradle, undisturbed by our revelry.

"My friends," Léon then continued, "the emotion of this night of excitement and friendship has affected me so strongly, that I wish to open my heart, too long sealed up. There is a remorse in my life, and the name of this remorse is Anna! I was this poor girl's first love, and I have ill requited her! She was a child without principles or reason. It was for me, a man, to give her a heart and a brain. I did not know

it, because I could not. I thought my intellect too great to perform a good act of which I should have reaped the reward. I was at an age of high ambitions, bitter rancors, and foolish illusions. Why should I, I asked myself, devote myself to the happiness of one woman, when all the others ought to give it to me? Thus reasons presumptuous youth. I have reached maturity, and I see that in other stations women are no better than in ours. If they have more prudence and reserve, they have less devotion and sincerity. The faults that Anna has committed she would not have committed, if I had been patient and generous; now this deluded girl is a tender mother, so tender, so courageous, so touching, that I pardon all! If I returned to the world, to marry under these conditions would be ridiculous and scandalous. In the life we lead, it is a good action; whence I conclude that for me the theatre will be more moral than society. So I remain there, and bind myself to it indissolubly. Bellamare, you have often reproached me for having profited by the weakness of a child, and scorned her for that weakness which ought to have attached me to her. I would not accept this reproach. I feel now that it was merited, that it was the source of my misanthropy. ·I intend to free myself from it; I will marry Anna. She thinks that I have had a return of love for her, but that it is not serious, and that my continual suspicions will render our union impossible. She will not permit me to think the child is mine, to punish me for doubting her. Ah well, I love the child, and I will rear it. I will do justice to the mother. I swear to you, in her absence, my friends, so that you may serve as vouchers for me with her; I swear to marry Anna — ”

“ And you will do well,” cried Bellamare, “for I am sure, for my part, that she has always loved you. — Come!” said he, addressing the rising day, which, mingled oddly with the moonlight, sent a broad blue glimmer across the flowers and tapers, “shine forth, young caressing day, the fairest of my life! All my friends happy, and I — I! Impéria! my saint, my beloved, my daughter! we are then at last to act for art!— Listen, Lawrence, if I accept the capital that you lend me —”

“ Pardon,” said Lawrence, “ I hope that this time there will be no question of restitution. I know you, Bellamare; the perpetual obstacle of your life is your conscience. With a smaller capital than that I put into your hands you would have retired from business, if you had not always owed friends whom you would not ruin. With me you cannot have that fear. My offering will not even inconvenience me; and if it did a little, if I should have to curtail something of my too large expenditures — You have given me three years of a well-occupied life, which has carried away all the froth from my youth, and there now remains to me only the love of an ideal of which you are the most persuasive and persuaded apostle and professor. You have formed my taste, elevated my ideas, taught me devotion and courage. All that is young and gener-

ous in my soul I owe to you. Thanks to you, I did not become a sceptic. Thanks to you, I have a worship for the true, a confidence in goodness, a power of loving. If I am still worthy to be the choice of an adorable woman, it is because, through a life wild as a dream, you have always said to me, ‘ My child, when the angels pass in the dust that we raise, let us kneel, for there are angels, whatever they may say!’ So I am your debtor forever, Bellamare, and it is not with one or two years of my income that I can repay you. Money does not discharge such debts. I understand; you wish to follow art and not the profession; ah well, my friend, recruit a good company to complete your own, and act good pieces always. I do not think that you will make a fortune; there are so many people who love the ignoble! but I know you; you will be happy in your competence, when you can use good literature and apply a good method, without sacrificing anything to the exigencies of the receipts.”

“ You are right!” answered Bellamare, radiant and affected. “ You have understood me, and my dear associates understand me. O ideal of my life! to be no longer forced to earn money for my daily bread! To be able at last to say to the public, ‘ Come to school, my little friend. If the beautiful bores you, go to bed. I have ceased to be the slave of your vulgar sons. We are not going to barter twaddle for bread. We have bread, even as yourself, my master; and we would far sooner eat it dry than soak it in the smoke of your mental grossness. Little public, you who bring great profits, learn that Bellamare's theatre is not what you think. We can do without you when you sulk; we can wait for your return, when a taste for the true has come back to you. It is a duel between us and you. You make a strike? So be it! We shall play still better before fifty persons of culture than before a thousand undiscriminating geese! But see on the ceiling that red sunbeam, that makes all our faces, weary with the past, look wan and pale, but which, descending speedily upon our foreheads, shall make them resplendent with the joys of hope! It is the rising sun, it is the splendor of the true, it is the dazzling foot-light which ascends from the horizon, to illuminate the stage where all humanity is about to play the eternal drama of its passions, its struggles, its triumphs, and its downfalls. But we, since we are actors, are birds of night! We return into the shades of nothingness when the earth stirs and awakes; but here at last is the lovely morning which smiles on us as on real beings, and says to us, 'No, you are not spectres; no, the drama that you have acted this night is not an empty fiction; you have all

seized your ideal, and it will not escape you again. You can go to sleep, my poor artisans of fancy; you are now men like the others; you have strong affections, serious duties, durable joys. You have not bought them too dearly nor too late; look me in the face, I am life, and you have at last a right to life!'"

Bellamare's enthusiasm took possession of us all, and there was no one there who did not think that happiness lies in the consciousness we have of it, and by no means in the way the future keeps its promises. I was as excited as the rest, I who had had no other part or merit in all this adventure than that of devoting myself for some days to hastening and assuring the happiness of others.

When I found myself alone again, several days after, in the prosaic chain of my nomadic life, this supper of actors in the ancient monastery of Bertheville seemed like a dream to me, but like so singular and so romantic a dream, that I promised myself surely to fulfil my pledge to Lawrence, and to repeat it with the same guests as soon as circumstances would permit.

THE END.

Cambridge : Electrotyped and Printed by Welch, Bigelow, & Co.

www.ingramcontent.com/pod-product-compliance
Lightning Source LLC
Chambersburg PA
CBHW032016010726
47493CB00007B/2432